I0556966

For Phonekeo

Fearnomena

Kieran Wiesenberg

Fearnomena is a work of fiction. Names, characters, places, and incidents are either the product of the author's imagination or are used fictitiously. Any resemblance to actual events, locales, or persons, living or dead, is entirely coincidental.

Copyright © 2023 by Kieran Wiesenberg Productions LLC

All rights reserved.

No portion of this book may be reproduced in any form without written permission from the publisher or author, except as permitted by U.S. copyright law.

For rights inquiries, permissions, or additional information, please contact:

Kieran Wiesenberg Productions LLC

PO Box 11

Henrietta, NY 14467

info@kieranwiesenberg.com

www.kieranwiesenberg.com

Fearnomena / Kieran Wiesenberg. — 1st edition v2

ISBN 979-8-9860007-2-5

Cover illustration and design by Kieran Wiesenberg

Casper

Something was bugging Casper. He couldn't put his finger on it, but he thought it probably had something to do with fourteen.

The number, the word, the idea itself, he and fourteen had never gotten along. It had been fourteen agonizing days he'd spent in the hospital after breaking his leg on a ski trip to Boriban. Fourteen times he'd been stung by stupor wasps at Ierra. Fourteen credits he'd had on him when a couple of thugs at a Meumyn spaceport decided to jump him and take the measly amount for themselves. He'd been fourteen months old when his mom died, and fourteen years when his dad followed suit. No matter where Casper went, fourteen seemed to follow, bringing with it always some degree of despair or bad luck. The irony was not lost on him that he'd been born on Endsember 14th, Endsember being the 14th month in the Laynillion standard year.

Today was Endsember 14th, and Casper was turning 41, a fateful age if ever there was one, but that was not all. This was his 14th time aboard the Phenomena 7, a heat-powered shipping freighter designed for transporting goods across the galaxy, and his second time as its captain. Phenomena 7, second shift as captain, the math there was not hard. More, this specific job had them finishing up with a transport from Meumyn to Qlaus, two planets that just so happened to be 1378 parmins apart. 1400 if you rounded up.

And there it was again.

Casper liked to think that he wasn't overly superstitious, but then, when it came to fourteen, his now 41 years had taught him to at least be wary. Nothing bad had happened so far, but then, as he glanced at his watch, saw that it was a quarter to 2:00—14:00 in standard—he knew that the day was still young.

He turned his eyes to the bridge window, to the vast galaxy which lay beyond, and to the rocks. They were in the Strap system, currently making their slow way through one of the biggest asteroid fields east of the Cipher Belt. Everywhere Casper looked, the gray giants loomed, each one floating in its own unique trajectory as the ship maneuvered, automatically, between them. Autonav was a godsend. Could Casper have piloted himself? Sure. Could probably have shaved a couple minutes off the ETA while he was at it. But why bother? The autonav would get them where they were going, and in the meantime, he could relax.

That Casper's relaxation often involved his standing on the bridge itself, the ship's controls ever within reach, and beckoning, was his own problem.

He glanced down at the autonav monitor and immediately wished he hadn't. Their ETA was fourteen hours and fourteen minutes. If Casper needed any more convincing that it was a bad idea for him to pilot today, that was it.

Turning from the bridge, he made his way to the rec room instead. Catching his reflection in the steel double doors, he was taken by the sight of himself. His beard had grown long. He always let it go on big jobs like this, and always he was startled by how fast it came in. He didn't much like the look of it when it got to this length, thought it made him come off too fierce. Add it to his large frame and he just looked like a big hairy brute.

He tried a smile in the reflection, hoping maybe it would take some of the edge off. It didn't. Only served to make him look scarier, if not goofy as all get out. He let it fall with a sigh. *Looks like frowning it is.* He punched a button on the door control panel and stepped through into the rec.

The whole crew was there like he knew they'd be. It was a good crew, this one. A rare crew. That they were all in the rec room together, rather than wasting the time away in their rooms was proof enough of that, and that was no small thing. Too many crews Casper had worked on where nobody gave a shit about anybody, didn't even try to pretend, and made the job all the tougher for it. The way Casper saw it, galaxy transport was tough enough as it is. No reason to go and make it any harder. Better to do it with a good crew around you. A good team. And Casper's crew was as good a team as any. They'd been together a few months already and, Casper wasn't ashamed to admit, he was hoping they'd stay together a few more.

Lumen was the first to look up, pulling herself out of the handheld game she was playing long enough to smile at him. "Sup, Cap," she said, prompting eyes and greetings from the rest.

"Hey," Casper said. "How's everyone doing?"

"Not so good," came Parenti, face scrunched behind his glasses. He sat at the end table across from Margo, a chess game in between them.

"I take it Margo has yet to end her winning streak?" Casper said, crossing his arms and leaning back against the door frame.

"Never," said Margo, flashing a devilish grin which, upon landing on Casper, softened. Casper returned it but, remembering how goofy he must have looked, quickly turned away.

"Man, Parenti was our only hope," moaned Lumen. "Our last chance to stop Margo's bloody conquest." She let her fist fall dramatically on the table, making an empty coffee mug jump and startling Felix who sat, ever quietly, beside her.

Parenti turned at this, ghostly blue eyes piercing Lumen from under raised brows. "*Was?*" he repeated. "I certainly hope you're not implying that I've already lost."

"Only as much as the board is, my guy. That game is *over*."

He sneered, returned his eyes to the game. "We'll see."

While Parenti contemplated his next move, Margo turned to Casper. "We got some news from HQ this morning."

"We did?" Casper said, tilting his head to one side. He hadn't remembered seeing anything.

"Oh yes, and it was very important. Something to do with today's date..." She shot him a knowing smile and Casper felt himself tense up. He didn't like where this was going.

With a rehearsed movement, all four of them suddenly withdrew previously concealed coffee mugs, placed them upside down on their heads, and in unison cried: *"Happy Birthday, Casper!"*

Though he tried his best to keep it at bay, that goofy smile eventually broke free. "You guys...how did you know?"

"Turns out the ship keeps a log of every crewmate's date of birth," said Parenti. "I was doing an inspection this morning when yours came up as a little notification." He was grinning now. "There's an intercom message and everything. Check it out."

He rolled his chair from the end table to the corner, to where the rec room's computer sat. After tapping a few keys, the room was suddenly filled with a blue light and the three-note jingle that played before every intercom message. What followed was the robotic voice of the ship's computer.

"Happy Birthday, Casper," it said. Above each door, the same message rolled by in the electronic script of the text box.

"Betrayed by my own ship," Casper said, smiling even wider.

A light punch to his shoulder put Lumen at his side. "C'mon, Cap," she said, giving him a few more jabs. "You just wasn't gonna tell us?"

"I wasn't planning on it, no," Casper said, blocking the incoming blows with his forearm. She ended her assault and Casper lowered his arms. "I tend not to celebrate it too much when it comes around."

Margo's smile suddenly faded. "Oh, I'm sorry," she said. "I hope this all wasn't too much then. If we'd known—"

"No, no," Casper said, raising a hand. "Don't apologize. This was...this was great." He looked down. "I think the reason I tend not to celebrate is because I tend not to have anyone to celebrate with. At least not usually." His eyes came back up and he frowned. "Are those...coffee mugs?"

"Yessir!" said Lumen, standing tall.

"It would appear," muttered Parenti.

Margo adjusted hers where it sat on her head, her smile returned. "We didn't have time to get any actual birthday hats so I figured these were the closest thing."

Casper felt movement behind him and turned to find Felix, arms raised, bestowing him with a coffee mug birthday hat of his own. "Happy birthday, Cap," he said, dark eyes shining behind his long hair.

"Thanks, Felix," he said, pulling the young man into a one-armed embrace. "And thank you all. Once we get back to Qlaus, I'm buying everyone a round."

The collective cheer that followed was in turn followed by a pinging from the corner computer. Without dropping the still-unmoved rook between his fingers, Parenti rolled his chair back to the terminal.

"What is it?" Casper asked.

"Motion sensor tripped in the cargo bay," he said. A few taps on the keyboard turned the desktop screen into a live feed from the bay's camera. Positioned in the upper left-hand corner of the great room, the picture showed the hundreds of crates they'd picked up over the course of the job.

Casper craned his neck forward, squinting to get a better look. "See anything?"

"No," Parenti said after watching a moment longer. "Must be out of angle." He turned back to Casper, pushing his glasses up from where they'd slipped down the bridge of his nose. "Want me to go check it out?"

Casper shook his head. "I'll go. Odds are it's just one of those decking pallets again. Damn things are always breaking."

"I can help clean up if there's a spill," Parenti offered again, inching closer to the bay door.

"I'll manage," Casper said, raising a hand. He used it to point at the end table. "You've got a chess game to worry about."

Parenti looked back to the board, seeming to deflate as he did. "Right."

"You could always forfeit," Margo suggested cheerfully.

Parenti immediately pulled himself back to the table, a steely determination filling his eyes. "Never."

Smiling again, Casper strode to the opposite double doors, stopping only as his momentum threatened to pull the coffee mug birthday hat off his head. Frowning, he turned to one of the utility drawers adjacent and dug around some. Cutting a large rubber band in half, he used a roll of tape to fasten each of its ends to the edges of his mug. After giving the bottom a few tugs to ensure it was secure, he pulled the entire ensemble over his head and turned to face the crew.

"This dude..." Lumen said, bringing a palm to her face.

Margo was laughing. "You know you don't actually have to wear that, right?"

"Are you kidding me?" Casper said, grinning like a fool. "I'm keeping it on all day." And with that, he turned out of the rec room.

***

Though Casper wasn't usually one to celebrate his birthday, and certainly not for an age as unspectacular—and perhaps as ominous—as 41, he found that his current mood was trending toward the unusual.

He couldn't remember the last time someone had wished him a happy birthday in person, and even less the last time anyone had gone to the effort of surprising him for the occasion. Perhaps no one ever had.

No one until today, that is.

His crew had surprised him. And while coffee mug birthday hats maybe weren't much by way of surprises, to Casper, they were great. They were fantastic. And they'd put him in the mood to celebrate.

So, as he walked down the long halls of the Phenomena 7, Casper found himself seriously considering the prospect of cake.

Everyone liked cake. And so how better to celebrate one's birthday than by baking one? Casper decided there was no better way. He would bake it himself, of course. Wouldn't want anyone else toiling over something intended for the celebration of him, but it was about more than that too. It would be his thank you to his crew not only for their birthday wishes, but also for a job well done. They were at the tail end of what had been a long and arduous job, and while he'd already invited everyone to drinks, he doubted adding cake to the bargain would hurt any.

Because after all, everyone liked cake.

It was decided then. Just as soon as he checked the cargo bay, he would return to the rec room and begin cake preparation. The pantry had all the ingredients he would need, and if he was lucky, he might just find some more elsewhere.

It was rare, but the Phenomena 7 sometimes transferred food stuffs. It had this job, tons of crates from Jezeben. And sometimes—though this was even rarer—those food stuffs were the crates that fell. Sometimes they'd fall and be fine, but other times they'd fall and shatter, throwing their contents all over the bay floor. A shame for the ISC, all dropped food was unsellable, contaminated, profit loss. For the crew that was transporting it, though? It was fair game. Somebody's got to eat it, right? Why not those who'd gone to the trouble of getting it?

Casper found himself daydreaming about a particular crate of copper nuts he remembered loading himself. He had no reason to believe that they'd been what had spilled, no reason to believe that he would be that lucky, and especially not on his birthday. But then, it had been an unusual birthday so far, and so maybe that was reason enough.

When he finally got to the bay, opened the double doors which led to the great warehouse of a room, the first thing that hit him was the cold.

Like winter on a frost planet, the air hit him fast, chilled him, sent the skin on his neck prickling with goosebumps.

Strange, he thought. *Temperature should be controlled.*

It got colder as he stepped through the threshold. He turned to the control panel next to the door and pulled up the thermostat. The set temperature was at 68 as usual. The actual temperature, however, was at 58.

Unusual.

Looking closer, Casper saw that the discrepancy was confined only to the cargo bay, though that didn't make him feel any better. If the cargo bay was losing heat, then it could mean there was a breach in the insulation system, one that, if left unattended, could quickly spread to the rest of the ship, slowing vital functions and eventually resulting in a full system shutdown. What they called a coldout on heat-powered ships like the Phenomena 7, and what could prove disastrous were it to happen in the middle of an asteroid field.

Casper turned around, his immediate instinct to return to the bridge for a full diagnostics check, but stopped himself. If there was an insulation breach, then only the diagnostics check would reveal it. But if it was something else, something like a crate of cryogens having spilled all over the bay, then only checking the aisles would reveal that. The motion sensors had been tripped, which meant that *something* had fallen. Casper decided he needed to figure out what.

There were six aisles in all, and the trouble came from each one being about twenty-five yards long. Worse, they were full, filled with an entire job's worth of freight, those brown and gray boxes stacked near all the way to the bay's high ceiling. It made it so that being in one aisle made it impossible to see into the next. Made it so that finding a dropped crate required you to walk the complete length of every single one.

Casper was about halfway down the second aisle when he got the bright idea to radio back to the crew, and about three-fourths of the way down when he realized he couldn't.

He didn't have his communicator.

Perplexed for a moment, memory soon caught up with him, stinging like those stupor wasps back on Ierra as it did. Casper didn't much like carrying his gun around. Not in the field and especially not on the ship. Double especially not on Endsember 14th if he could help it. He always thought it'd be the death of him. Either he'd sit down wrong and shoot himself or the thing would just spontaneously combust, given his bad luck. Superstitious, maybe, but what was the harm? Now he knew. In taking the weapon off his belt he'd done the same with his communicator, leaving him now both unarmed and unreachable.

It wasn't a huge deal, only meant that he'd need to be quick about finishing his inspection of the bay. The quicker he could deal with whatever had triggered the motion sensor, the quicker he could deal with the temperature. Rounding the penultimate aisle, he upped his pace.

It wasn't until he got to the very last aisle that Casper found something amiss. About halfway down the length of it, a single shipping crate sat apart from the rest. Cockeyed and busted, it seemed to have fallen from the adjacent row, the impact enough to have knocked the lid loose. From where Casper stood some twenty feet away, he saw only a shadowy veil of what lay within.

Slowing his advance, Casper did a mental recall of the job's pickups. Had there been anything noxious? The outside of the box gave no indication of hazardous material, but then, when dealing with otherworldly imports, Casper found it best to always be extra cautious. Another moment and he came to his conclusion. No, there hadn't been anything toxic on this run, nothing that he could remember at least. Just in case, he activated the mask portion of his exosuit. No sense in taking needless risks, and especially not today. Seconds later, his mouth and nose were protected, the microfibers of his suit collar having expanded to cover them both.

At maybe four feet in length, four in width, and six in height, the crate was big. One of the bigger pieces of the entire shipment, and there were some monsters. The big crates usually meant big bucks. Sometimes they'd get cheap furniture, yeah, but most times the big ones were appliances. High end refrigerators and ovens and such. They were typically as heavy as they were expensive, meaning that loading a new one on was about as painful as trashing a broken one. Luckily, the crate in question was none of the above. Big as it was, it didn't hold an appliance, but a plant.

Casper remembered now. They had loaded a ton of plants back on Ignelin. Trees, shrubs, flowers, just about everything you could think of, and practically an entire forest's worth of it all. Something about the soil going bad. Casper wasn't too sure. He'd let Margo oversee it, her being the Phenomena

7's resident plant lover and knowing best how to transport them along with the rest.

The thought of Margo brought Casper's hand to his hip, to the communicator that still wasn't there, thinking to radio her about the fall. She'd know best how to remedy anything that had gotten discombobulated, if anything even had. But then, as his fingers scratched the leather of his empty belt, Casper remembered that it would have to wait. Until she could get down here and take a look for herself. Or, better yet, until he brought it up for her to do so. Casper thought she might appreciate that.

He'd found himself thinking a lot about things Margo might appreciate lately, and also about the things he knew she did. Getting to know her over the past few months had been a real highlight of this most recent job, one that Casper hoped would continue into the months that came after. If not by way of the next job then by something else. By something more, he hoped. He hadn't exactly asked her out yet, had never really felt right doing so, his being the captain and her technical superior and all, but they talked a lot. Talked about as much as two people can, being cooped up in a spaceship for all that time. It had been great, though Casper could tell she was waiting, just as he was. Waiting for the job to be over, for all the titles and responsibilities and obstacles to be out of the way. Waiting for when they could really begin whatever it was they were going to try. It had been a long wait, though they'd found ways to pass the time. By talking, by smiling, and, Casper supposed, by nursing fallen plant crates.

Squatting down to get a good grip on the thing, he stopped when he heard a sound.

There weren't many sounds aboard a ship like the Phenomena 7. With the computer in autonav, the octa-core engine hummed so softly as to not be humming at all. Besides that, there were only a few more typical noises. The sliding of the steel double doors, the pinging of the computers, the whirring of the heat and oxygen systems. You got to know all of them after a while, and with the great silence of space being the unflinching alternative, you got to relying on them.

The sound Casper heard was like none of these, however. Not a ship sound, but something more organic. Something like a buzzing.

Something like a bug.

Casper sighed. This was not the first time a bug had infiltrated the Phenomena 7's cargo, and though Casper would try his damndest to prevent it, he also knew it would not be the last. Those tiny bastards always found a way. That they should be so small yet prove so massive a nuisance always amazed him. And they were a nuisance. Bugs had the potential to ruin whole shipments of cargo. What they couldn't chew through they'd lay eggs in, and sometimes they'd do both. Then there was the threat of eco-invasion. Introduce the wrong bug to the right planet through an infested shipment, and you could doom an entire ecosystem. Of course, precautions were taken to prevent that kind of thing, but they were imperfect at best. Even if someone did figure out some foolproof way of getting rid of them, Casper doubted it would've mattered. Bugs were worse than fools, and they always *always* found a way.

Listening hard, it didn't take him long to zero in on where it was. The buzzing came from inside the crate, from some shadowy crevice beneath the plant. For a second, Casper considered jamming the lid back on, trapping the bastard in there and forgetting about it, but he knew better. No lid could keep the squirmy things contained for long. Better just to kill it, before it could reproduce and do the same to the cargo.

Casper gripped the plant tight in one hand, readying his other in a fist just above. He'd always preferred punching to slapping when it came to this kind of deal. He found it was more effective, and more personal too. Let the little shit know that what was coming was going to hurt, and that you meant it to.

A second later he was ripping the plant from the crate, looking to pummel whatever was left over, though what he saw made him freeze. Where he'd been expecting to find just one bug there was an entire bunch. And they were the biggest, blackest, gnarliest bugs Casper had ever seen.

He found himself staring dumbstruck. There had to be about ten of them down there—

"No, not ten. Look closer."

"What the—?" Casper said, whipping his head around.

He'd heard a voice just then, only, there was no one there.

"No, not there," it said again, and it seemed to come from right below him. *"The bugs, Casper. Look at the bugs."*

"Huh?" Casper said, looking down, one hand still clutching the plant, the other still cocked by his shoulder.

"Good. Now count them, Casper. Count how many there are."

Casper found himself doing so. Not because he wanted to really, but because he couldn't help it. Because he had a horrible suspicion.

"Well, how many are there?"

Swallowing hard, Casper spoke more to himself than to the voice. "Fourteen."

"Very good. Now...where are you off to?"

Casper had gotten up, had started to run. The temperature drop made sense now. The flies, the number, all of it. And the more cold air filled his lungs, the more Casper knew he needed to get out of there, and fast.

Somewhere behind him, the buzzing had grown louder.

"Going so soon?" said the voice. It was much louder now, and it seemed to come at him from everywhere, seemed to intermingle with the bug-sounds behind him.

Casper didn't look back.

He had just turned out of the final aisle, to the straightaway that led back to the entrance when something crashed into him. When some*things* crashed into him. The force was enough to knock him to the floor.

"I'm talking to you," snarled the voice, right on top of him now.

Casper turned around then, could put it off no longer. He turned and saw what the voice had become, what its buzzing had amassed into. Not just one bug, or ten, or even fourteen, but *hundreds.*

They hovered just before Casper, together a great, black, squirming ball. Their collective drone was enough to drown under, their collective mass liable to do the same. Casper met them with hard eyes.

"I know what you are," he said. "And I'm not afraid."

The bugs seemed to change then, seemed to lose their shape and morph into some gaseous blue. Into what they truly were.

"No?" said the voice, and in an instant the bugs were whole again. They broke away from the singular blob, splitting into two halves of a shape more distinct. Of a number.

Fourteen.

"Are you sure?"

Casper was backing away now. Not because he was afraid, but because he needed to get out. Needed to lock this thing in the cargo bay and dispel it before it could get to the rest of the ship. Before it could get to the rest of the crew.

"Yes," Casper said, still backing. "I'm not afraid because what you show can't hurt me. Because it's not *real.*"

Speaking these last words from the heart, the effect was instantaneous. In seconds the great bug-numbers were gone, were dissipating in a cloud of dark blue smoke, revealing for an instant the silhouette of what lay underneath.

Casper turned before he saw it completely. He didn't need to. He knew what this thing was, and he knew what it could do. Any more time spent looking would just lower his chances of escape.

He'd nearly made it to the doors when a terrible chill ran through him, made him falter. By the time he'd steadied himself, he looked up to find the intruder standing in the threshold, blocking his escape.

"You really aren't afraid?" it asked, and it was in its true form now, small black eyes peering out of a great blue skull.

Casper shook his head, missing his density gun more every minute.

"Of anything?" it said, and its words were followed by such a rush of cold that Casper was forced to close his eyes, sniff back a now-runny nose.

Some smoke had appeared then, its dark blue coils curling around the thing's head in such a way as to obscure it. As to suggest that it might become something new.

It didn't work.

Casper had seen it now. Had seen it for what it truly was. Its illusions wouldn't work on him anymore. No matter how hard it tried. And no matter how cold it got.

Casper took a step forward, planning out the best way to take it down without a gun. It may have been partially gaseous, but those long blue limbs looked solid enough to touch. Thin enough to break too, if it came to that.

Casper thought that it might.

"Interesting," it said, seemingly unbothered by Casper's approach. *"You might be my first. The first I couldn't freeze."*

Casper kept on, cracking his knuckles as he pressed forward.

"Luckily, there are other means." It stepped backwards then, through the threshold and shut the double doors from the other side.

A second more and Casper would've been through too, but the thing was quick, and it locked him out before he could cross.

In an instant he was at the adjacent control panel, jamming in the code to unlock, but it wouldn't go. He looked up to see the intruder's blue face in the window, no doubt overriding his inputs from the opposite side.

He slammed his fist against the glass. The make was space rated, so he knew it wouldn't break. He slammed anyway.

"So much anger, so little fear," said the intruder, and it almost sounded sad. Casper watched as it turned to its own control panel, began entering in something new.

A loud sound from the front of the bay was followed by a three-note jingle and another message from the intercom.

"Cargo bay doors unlocked," it said.

Casper's eyes went wide. "No—"

He tried to grab for the control panel, but it was already out of reach. He was already floating away. The bay doors were opening now, subjecting the room to space and killing the gravity lock. All around him, Casper watched as the thousand crates of cargo rose, weightlessly, from where they'd once sat. Casper watched as he did the same.

At zero gravity, the only thing preventing him and everything else from being sucked out into the void was the storm door. A translucent energy screen, the storm door was primarily used to keep things in while the actual doors were open. Every once in a while though, it was used to get things out. And it was as easy as flipping a switch on the control panel.

"Goodbye, Casper," said the intruder, and it flipped the switch to deactivate the storm door.

Casper had but seconds to react.

As he was pulled inexorably out of the gaping hole in the ship and into the space beyond, he activated the full-body function of his exosuit. Made only of nanonylon microfibers, the suit wasn't really made for space. It could take the atmospheric extremes of planets like Lagustun and Gliir, sure, but the extremes of space were something else entirely.

It would keep him breathing though. Would keep his eyes from being immediately sucked out of his head. And so Casper activated it anyway.

An instant later he was out, one of the thousand pieces of expelled cargo, all of it just floating amongst the asteroids.

The cold hit him immediately, and hard. Harder than it should have. The click of his suit locking a second late explained it, and it sent more than just physical chill down Casper's spine.

The suit locking a second late meant a second he'd spent with it unlocked, partially exposed to the harsh elements of space. A second wasn't much. On a planet like Lagustun or Gliir, it might not have even mattered. But in space, a second could prove vital.

Could prove fatal.

Casper could already feel himself getting sleepy, could feel the suit trying to warm him, using up its energy and depleting his oxygen supply in the process. There was nothing he could do about it. Nothing but think. Nothing but wonder what had gone wrong.

Had he been too slow?

No, he'd activated it quick enough. The microfibers should have closed. Should have stretched the span of his body and locked just like they always did.

So why hadn't they?

A large metallic crate revealed the answer. As it floated by, Casper caught his reflection in its glossy surface, caught his head looking abnormally large, and more so than would be expected from the distorted surface. It looked like something was on his head, something small with a distinct and familiar shape.

Something like a coffee mug.

It was then Casper realized that he'd never taken the makeshift birthday hat off his head. It was then he realized that, it being of a significant size, it would've caused the microfibers to stretch just a bit farther, and to take just a bit longer to cover him completely.

A bit too long.

As he watched the metallic crate steal away his reflection for the cosmos beyond, Casper hated to think that his birthday gift might have been the death of him. But think it he did. He couldn't help himself.

And just when he'd thought his luck was turning around.

For no reason he could explain or really knew, Casper began to count. Maybe it was to keep him from thinking bad thoughts, or maybe it was just because he had nothing better to do. Either way, count is what he did. Counting away his last moments. Seeing how high he could get.

He got to thirteen before his lips stopped moving. Before the cold seeped in and shut his drooping eyes for good.

It seemed fourteen hadn't gotten him in the end.

Had he still been able to, he might have laughed.

Margo

Margo thought he must've been joking.

She'd given much lenience, granted plenty of opportunities, and even made a few glaring mistakes of her own, any of which could have easily been her downfall, been the lynchpin needed to turn the tables and tip those black and white scales against her.

Unfortunately, Parenti hadn't seen any of them.

It wasn't that he was bad at chess. Compared to opponents like Lumen and Casper—especially Casper—the lanky computer-head had definitely given her the toughest run for her money. He was smart. He had potential. But he kept making mistakes.

The latest took the form of his rook. He'd moved it up in an adept play that threatened her final knight while simultaneously putting pressure on her queen. What it failed to account for was her bishop halfway across the board, all but hidden in the black space it occupied, uncloaking just long enough to fly beneath her fingers and eliminate the attacking piece in one fell swoop.

Margo thought he must've been joking. Making bone-headed moves on purpose to either level the playing field or throw the game completely. Now she knew that he wasn't. It was written in the lines of shock and frustration all over his face. Margo couldn't help but be glad to see them.

Her playing field needed no leveling.

Parenti's tightened features were suddenly bathed in a blue glow. The three-note jingle played and the rec room was suddenly filled by another message from the intercom.

"Cargo bay doors unlocked," it said, and not a second later, "Cargo bay storm door deactivated."

Lumen looked up from her handheld. "Um?"

Margo already had her communicator in her hand. "Everything okay, Casper?" She let the trigger go, let the silence yawn out after the static.

"He didn't radio anything about a dispel, right?"

A shake of the head from Lumen. Parenti was already at the corner computer, clacking loudly on the keyboard.

"I can't see anything," he said.

"What?"

"The feed is down," he said, moving to the side so Margo could see the screen. The readout was black. "It happens occasionally when the storm door is opened. Messes with the temperature and forces the camera into a hard reboot."

"Casper, do you copy?" Margo was saying again, clutching her communicator tighter than usual.

"No radio," Felix said quietly.

Margo whipped around. "What?"

The young man seemed to shrink away from all the new eyes on him, looked down and mumbled even quieter.

"Casper, he...he didn't have his radio on him. Didn't have his gun either."

Margo regarded the young man for a moment. He was a strange kid, Felix, a sharp kid. He didn't talk much, but he didn't miss much either.

What he'd seen decided it.

"I'm going down there," she said, striding toward the double doors. And before anyone could say anything different, she was out, making her way to Casper.

***

The walk from the rec room to the cargo bay was a long one. The Phenomena 7 being as big as it was, it was a long walk filled by even longer, gray hallways. There were some windows, though, so it wasn't all bad. As she walked, Margo found her head filling with thoughts of Casper—it had a funny way of doing that lately—and so it certainly wasn't all bad.

She liked him; that much was obvious. The only thing more obvious was that he liked her back. And that was *obvious.*

They hadn't done anything yet. *He* hadn't done anything yet, though she knew he wanted to. And she knew she wanted to too.

They'd known each other for a few months now, since the start of the job. A long time to know someone and not do anything, especially considering their rapport had been near-immediate, but then, they'd been working. There was a time when Margo would have been more impatient. There was a time when she might have viewed this delay as a sign of ineptitude if not plain disinterest. Indeed there was a time when she would likely have already taken steps to accelerate the process herself, work or not.

But then, this was a different time.

Margo wasn't twenty anymore, as the sight of Felix so often reminded her, or even twenty-six, as the sight of Lumen so often did the same. She was thirty-nine this year, and while the twenty-year-old Margo may have appreciated—and perhaps expected—a certain degree of speed and vigor, the soon-to-be forty-year-old Margo appreciated something else. They were taking their time with each other, that was what was important. She figured it was the mature thing to do. And Margo was certainly mature enough.

Still, she found that the end of the job could not come soon enough.

It was the responsibilities and taboos of their working relationship that had put so many invisible walls between them, ones that Margo looked forward to breaking down as soon as possible. Casper had invited them all to drinks upon landing. She hoped he'd make his move then. And if he didn't, she would make hers.

Because she was mature enough for that too.

The more she thought about it, the more her mood began to shift. The intercom message back in the rec room had been unsettling, had made her fear the worst when paired with Casper's radio silence. Luckily, fear was all it had been. Margo was sure of it. Casper was fine, and the closer she got to the cargo bay, the more convinced of it she became. Still, she found herself picking up her pace, zipping her exosuit up to the collar as she did. It had gotten cold all of the sudden.

She was nearly through the last hall when something emerged from around the incoming corner, made her stop dead.

It didn't come all the way out. Just fingertips and the sliver of a head, space enough for a single eye to see out, peek at her. Space enough for the corner of a mouth to peek out too, all red paint over white, grin at her.

Margo felt her stomach drop as recognition settled in. Even the small portion she saw was unmistakable. This was a clown. And worse, it was a clown she knew.

As if on cue, it moved then, unfolded itself from its hiding space and stepped entirely into the hallway. Its long pin-striped legs took it to the ceiling and beyond, forced it to hunch its head forward. Its long, polka-dotted arms followed suit, forcing its hands to curl back at the ground. Its suit was disheveled in the worst way, its hair and nose as red as ever.

As red as Margo remembered.

"Hello, Margo," it said, grin wide.

Margo had her density gun up in an instant, safety off, aimed straight at the head.

"Who are you?" she demanded.

The clown mocked surprise, shifted back and put its too-long-arms up.

"Whoa there, Margo, take it easy. Don't you recognize me?" Keeping one arm up, it used the other to point at a hastily scrawled name tag with a too-long-finger. "It's me, Dresserdoc!"

The name alone was enough to make Margo's stomach churn.

Dresserdoc the clown, one half of Dresserdoc and Bobinski, the beloved clown duo. An old-school partnership turned galaxy-wide franchise, Dresserdoc and Bobinski were as household a name as galactic characters could be. For years the two had been engaging in slapstick hijinks to the enjoyment of millions. Everyone loved them.

Everyone except Margo.

She'd never been one for slapstick, and even less for clowns. That her three older brothers had practically idolized the duo growing up had made them all the less appealing. Worse, they'd always frightened her. Something about the makeup, the smiling, the fatsuit for Bobinski, the stilts for Dresserdoc, it had all just seemed so unnatural. Uncanny in the worst possible way. She'd had consistent nightmares about them throughout childhood, and about Dresserdoc specifically. Nightmares that seemed to have just now become real.

"If this is some kind of joke, you'd better say so right now," she said, lowering her aim to the clown's chest without loosening her grip.

She kept looking for something familiar, something beyond the getup. Something that would tell her it was all just a prank. Parenti in a wig. Casper on a pair of stilts. Something to prove that it wasn't real.

The closer she looked, however, the realer it became.

This was no man in a wig, or even on stilts. This was worse than the Dresserdoc she remembered, the one that, though frightening, had always just been a man in costume, a character, a fake. This was no fake. This was Dresserdoc made real.

This was Dresserdoc from her nightmares.

"See? Now you remember," said the clown, taking a step forward.

Without thinking, Margo took one back. She could feel her heart quickening in her chest now, and she cursed herself for her fear.

"Take another step and I shoot," she said, returning her aim to the clown's head.

Dresserdoc froze, though his grin never faltered.

"What do you want?" she demanded.

Again, the clown mocked surprise. "What do I want?" he repeated, pressing a long white finger into his chest, and his mouth curved into its widest smile yet. "Why, to eat you of course."

The shiver Margo had been holding back finally broke through, wracking her body enough to shake her arms, to shift the aim of her gun, and to give Dresserdoc a chance to close the distance.

He made it a single step before Margo shot him in the face.

Margo had fired her density gun in the field before on three occasions. The first at a Riidobeast on Gliir, the second at a Yutanolep on Cizzar, and the third during a cargo trade gone wrong on Loomslo. Them all being mellow incidents comparatively, she'd managed to keep the switch on stun for each. That was the nice thing about density guns. With a rotating knob that held ten different density settings, a shooter could determine the lethality of every single discharge. This being the fourth shot Margo had taken on the job, and the millionth she'd taken in her lifetime, it was the first she'd taken on a lethal setting.

It was also the first that hadn't worked.

Not for a lack of precision—Margo was a sharp-shooter, the sharpest on the Phenomena 7 and everyone knew it—the impact at least, had been good. Though she'd never shot anyone in the face before, she'd seen enough movies and TV shows to have an idea of what it looked like when it worked. And, at least initially, this one had.

Catching the clown right between the eyes, the space that in one second had been occupied by Dresserdoc's head was, in the very next second, occupied by an explosion of mush.

But the color was off.

The red-pink hues of typical blood spatter and brain matter were noticeably absent, replaced altogether by a procession of blue-blacks, ones that, in their content as much as their color, appeared markedly inhuman.

That settled it then. However the thing before Margo might have appeared, it was not a clown or even a human, but something else entirely. A fact underscored as the thing's imploded head began to reconstitute itself.

Coming together in a swirling motion of smoky blue gas, the restoration of Dresserdoc's grinning face was preceded in its final moments by his sick giggle.

"Hehehehehe," went the clown, mouth moving even before his lips had completely returned.

Margo was backing away now, desperately fighting the rising fear in her chest. Desperately fighting the cold too, that which seemed to have encased the hall in an icy grip. She knew they were connected now, the cold and the fear. Knew that the thing before her was responsible for both. Knew that if she stood a chance of getting out of here, that she'd need to resist.

"Figured it out, did you?" hissed Dresserdoc, and his voice was different now, was tinged with the tone of that which he truly was.

"I must say I'm impressed," he said, taking a step forward, and as he did his knuckles dragged along the ground behind him. *"Your captain was also quick on the draw."*

Margo froze in her retreat.

"What did you do to him?" she asked, voice deadly.

Dresserdoc only smiled.

"Why, the same thing I'm doing to you," he said, and through a gap in his grin emerged what looked like a great black fly. *"I showed him what he was most afraid of.*

"It wasn't much," the clown admitted, snatching the bug from the air with two long fingers. *"I had to resort to pet peeves. Superstitions. Not scary things on the outset, maybe."* He began to squeeze the fly, grinding it between his fingertips. *"But give them enough time and—"*

Margo shot him again, twice this time.

She wouldn't hear any more of it. She couldn't, not if she wanted to stand a chance. Dresserdoc may have been her worst fear, he who had haunted her nightmares since she was young, but the thought of something happening to Casper, the thought of losing him before she'd had a chance to have him, that was a nightmare totally new. One she'd had yet to wrestle with, and one she could not afford to now. She needed to keep her fear in check, needed to keep it from overpowering her, and from overpowering that which fed off it.

And so she'd shot him again, twice, though her shots had done nothing.

It wasn't that she'd missed—Margo never missed. She'd seen the blasts impact, had even seen them make the clown flinch. Though they hadn't hurt him this time. Hadn't blown him open and warranted reconstitution like they had before. Margo knew why. The pace of her heart told her with every beating repetition.

"It's no use, Margo," he said, taking another lurching step forward. *"You can't hurt me now. You're too afraid."*

"No—" Margo said, flinching as her heel hit the wall behind her. She was out of options now. Out of time. Out of will. Before her, the tall clown drew ever closer.

"Go ahead," he said, red lips curling back in impossible spirals. *"Say it. Admit how scared you are."*

"No!" Margo cried, scrunching her eyes shut. She didn't want to look at him anymore. She couldn't. But then, if she wanted to stand any chance, she knew she had to.

She knew it was the only way.

And so she forced herself to open her eyes, forced herself to look upon the monstrosity before her. He was but a few steps away now, the very thing of her nightmares, all laid out before her in stunning detail. She forced herself to keep looking. Forced herself to take it all in, to face it, and condense it down.

"I'm not scared of you," she said, glaring into the clown's dead eyes.

In response, Dresserdoc merely laughed and inched forward.

Margo ignored his laughs. "I'm not *scared* of you," she said again, and this time she lowered her density gun, and upon doing so noticed something different.

The clown's arms, previously long enough to drag on the ground behind it, looked shorter now. Its head too, previously mere inches from the ceiling, suddenly sat lower. It looked different as well. Less like a clown's head and more like something else. Something big and blue. Almost balloon-like.

It lasted for but an instant.

Upon taking another step closer, the thing closed the distance and immediately reverted to its previous form. Whatever momentary control Margo had held over her fear, it was lost through mere proximity. Dresserdoc was back, and he was upon her.

She tried raising her density gun again, but got only halfway before the clown caught it. She recoiled at the force of his grip, and also at the feeling. Icy.

"You're a lot like him, you know," he said, his whisper like frostbite in her ears. *"Your captain, he too was brave. It's not many who can face their fears like that. Who can look past the things I show them."*

Margo tried again at her gun hand, tried to jerk against the clown's grip, but found that it wouldn't move. The cold spot where he held her wrist had spread to her entire hand now, was quickly traveling up the rest of her arm. She felt herself shivering.

"Of course, he got farther than you, he who had so little to fear." Keeping one hand on her wrist, he brought the other to her face, caressed her cheek with his long white fingers. *"You never stood half as good a chance, you who have so much."*

Margo could see her breath now, could feel her face freezing beneath the clown's cold touch. Though she couldn't bite, her teeth still chattered. Though she couldn't blink, her eyes still filled with tears. She tried to speak.

"Eauhh...*Eaauhh!*"

"Shhhhhhhhhhhh," Dresserdoc hushed, bringing his finger to her lips. The length of it extended all the way to her forehead. *"Hush now. You'll be asleep soon.*

"Yours are my favorite, you know. Those fears that come from childhood. Those fears that fester, remaining even years later. A lifetime of fear. There's truly nothing like it."

Margo went numb then, and the world went with her. Both of them drifting into a cold, dead sleep. The last thing she saw was Dresserdoc's grinning face, and the last thing she felt was all the fear that had ever come with it.

Parenti

P arenti felt dirty. He had all morning. And if there was
one thing he despised more than anything in the world,
it was feeling dirty.

The reasons for this feeling, which were three altogether,
could each be attributed, at least in some capacity, to the
chess game.

There were the pieces, for one. Those germ collectors.
Things designed for the sole purpose of being clutched by
hundreds of grubby hands without respite. To think that
they spent the other half of their time shoved inside a dark
case, a spawning ground for unending multiplication, was
enough to make him shudder. He'd taken steps to sanitize
them of course. Had insisted on wiping down each and every
one before the game had even commenced. A barebones solution ever, unfortunately, imperfect. Even with his practiced hand, he was sure there were things missed. Those little
places in the design. Those tiny crevices where sat the king's
crown, the knight's eye, the castle's bailey. It was in these
places where the germs undoubtedly survived, lying in wait

to infect the next hand unfortunate enough to traipse their contaminated wares. A hand that just so happened to be Parenti's own.

Then there was the problem of his exosuit. Parenti was a sweater, and chronically so. It seemed no climate was mild enough to stop his palms from wetting, nor any other place on his body. Physical activity, of course, was the greatest contributor, though mental exertion was no relief. Parenti's pores did not discriminate. And neither did his exosuit. The suit absorbed perspiration automatically, stored it in the microfibers to be used later. As drinking water on hot planets, and as added insulation on cool ones. Useful features to be sure, ones that had even aided Parenti on many an extreme occasion. When it was life or death, Parenti took what he could get. When it wasn't, he found that the idea of drinking recycled sweat-water quickly turned repulsive.

Lastly, there was the state of the game itself. Parenti was losing, and badly at that. Grossly, at that. He wasn't sure exactly where or when he'd gone wrong, only that he'd been going the same way ever since. Perhaps he'd been going wrong since the very start. The sorry state of the board as it sat now certainly implied as much. Regarding the ugly affair before him, Parenti wasn't sure what he was more ashamed of, that he'd let it get to this point or that he'd let it drag out for this long. Perhaps both. Perhaps neither. Either way the solution was clear.

It was time to forfeit.

He decided he'd do so just as soon as Margo returned. It was the logical thing to do after all. No point in remaining on a sinking ship for pride's sake. The board could keep his pride. Parenti found the prospect of a shower much more enticing. He would have already gone had it not been bad etiquette to make a move in the absence of the other player—even if that move was one of forfeit. No, Parenti would end the game just as soon as Margo returned.

Until then, he conceded to sit in his filth.

As the fifteenth minute since her departure ticked grudgingly by, Parenti found himself becoming increasingly impatient. Checking the clock for the fifth time in a four-minute span, he was saved from the agony of seeing the time again by the blue light of an intercom message.

"Ship temperature 50 degrees," said the robotic voice of the ship's computer. "Ensure equilibrium."

Across the room, Lumen looked up from her handheld. "No wonder I'm cold. Isn't that supposed to be higher?"

Parenti nodded. "Internal standard is 68."

"So what's the deal?"

"The cargo doors most likely. Opening for a dispel is liable to make the temperature drop." He frowned at the scrolling readout. "Still..."

Parenti pulled his communicator to his lips, his practiced three-inch gap—who knew what kind of bacteria lurked in the receiver's filter fibers?—and pressed down on the trigger.

"Margo, Casper, do you copy? What's the status on the cargo doors?"

After the fading of the radio's crackle, the room was left eerily quiet. Staring in anticipation at the silent receiver, Parenti frowned harder. He turned to the corner computer.

"You got 'em on the cameras?" asked Lumen.

"Almost..." Parenti tapped thrice on the keyboard, jumped through three different feeds. He frowned as he came to the one that showed the cargo bay. It was still black. Strange. He tapped some more, looking for movement in the rooms and halls surrounding. He found it in the lower quadrant. "Got it," he said, bringing the picture to fullscreen.

"Both of them?"

"No, just Margo. Only..."

"What?" Lumen was up now, had draped herself over the back of his chair. Distancing himself ever so slightly from that side, Parenti nearly jumped as he bumped into Felix, who had soundlessly positioned himself on the other.

"What's going on here, Parenti?" Lumen asked, narrowing her eyes at the screen. "Why's she just standing there?"

"What?"

Taking a closer look at the screen, Parenti quickly forgot his discomfort.

Margo stood at the very end of the hallway, nearly out of the camera's view, but not quite. She stood perfectly still, arms at her side, ever neutral. Though, there was something odd about it. Something about the way she stood, about the posture, and about the implication. She'd drawn her density gun, though it hung dormant at her side, as still as the rest of her.

Parenti raised his communicator again. "Margo, do you copy? What's going on down there?"

As he spoke, Parenti watched Margo's image on the screen. He thought he saw her communicator blinking with his incoming message. Though she didn't move to answer it.

"Why isn't she answering?" asked Lumen. "She's got her communicator, doesn't she?"

"She does." Parenti nodded, continuing to frown at the screen. *Why did she draw her density gun?*

After another failed communication, Parenti had seen enough. "Okay, I'm going down there to check on her." He began to rise from his seat, but was stopped short by a hand on his shoulder.

"Wait," Felix said, staring hard at the screen. "Look there. In the corner."

Though normally averse to others touching him, Parenti was distracted from his ire by Felix's words. It was a rare thing that the young man spoke, and even rarer that he did so forcefully. So vehement was his tone now that Parenti had no choice but to listen.

Following Felix's eyes to the screen, he was glad he did.

There was something on the feed other than Margo now. Something other than her in the lower quadrant. Previously out of frame, it now slowly revealed itself, emerging from an adjacent hall and turning the pixels of the readout a dark, unmistakable blue.

Behind his glasses, Parenti's eyes went wide.

"What the hell is *that*?" asked Lumen, and she drew back some from the chair.

Shaken from his momentary stupor, Parenti was immediately hunched over the keyboard again, feverishly clacking new keys. He panned the camera downward, zoomed in and refocused, all of which only served to confirm his fears. Drawing back from the computer, he let his hands fall limply into his lap. "Not good."

"Not good?" Lumen was shaking the chair now. "What do you mean not good? What the hell—?"

Her words were cut short by new movement.

Previously standing with its back to the camera, the thing on the screen turned then, turned its big blue head around until it looked right into the zoomed-in lens, and with a thin mouth smiled.

A second later, the screen cut out, went as black as the feed from the cargo bay, and the sudden switch was enough to make Felix jump.

Parenti was immediately hunched over again. Pounding keys, he quickly switched to a third camera feed and saw black. He switched to a fourth and fifth and was met with the same result.

"Damn," he said.

"What? They're all down?"

Parenti hesitated to nod. It certainly looked that way. As he continued to surf through the feeds, they continued to come up blank, empty but for the digital glow of black nothing. "Come on, come on..." he said, clicking through faster.

Finally, he came to one that was still active, and not a moment too soon.

No sooner had the visual for another hall appeared than did the intruder do the same, its great blue limbs carrying it...south? No, the camera was flipped, which meant it was headed north. Headed for the rec room.

Parenti turned to the entrances. "Lock the doors," he said, turning back to the screen, though the new feed had gone black like the rest. "Lock them now!"

He didn't have to ask twice. Within seconds, the two sets of double doors which led out of the rec room had been shut and locked. Lumen gazed warily at those that she'd closed before turning back.

"Parenti...what's happening?"

Having already accessed the ship's data, Parenti found something that confirmed his worst fears. The internal temperature was 48 degrees now, two degrees lower than it had been not five minutes earlier. It seemed the temperature was dropping, and fast. He frowned at the blue-black screen before answering. There was no denying it now.

"The ship has been invaded," he said, turning to a wary-eyed Felix and Lumen. "We've been invaded...by an Amygdalom."

"A *what?*" Lumen said, squinting in confusion, though Felix's eyes went wide.

"An Amygdalom," Parenti repeated. "Class hydrozoa, order anthoathecata, of the family corynidae—"

"In English, Parenti," Lumen said.

Parenti frowned. "I'm afraid I have no clearer way of putting it—"

"A fearsucker," Felix said.

Now it was Parenti's turn to squint. "What did you say?"

The young man seemed to squirm at the prospect of speaking again so soon. "A fearsucker," he said. "That's...that's what they called them in my hometown."

"That's right." Parenti nodded, remembering. "I believe another common colloquial name is *fearnapper.*"

Lumen lit up at this. "Oh shit!" she said. "*That's* what that was?" Her features quickly fell back into confusion. "But wait, aren't those things supposed to look like your worst fear? All I saw was some kind of weird blue thing. Did you guys see some weird blue thing?"

"What we saw was the Amygdalom in its true form," Parenti explained. "Thanks to the camera, we were able to see it without it seeing us, without it *sensing* us, at least to a certain degree. Had we stood where Margo stood, we would have seen it as our deepest fears materialized."

"Yikes," Lumen said. "So, Margo...?"

"Seems to be in a fearstate. A type of fear-induced coma, its symptoms are similar to that of hypothermia. A climate manipulator, the Amygdalom chills the body of its victim until it has no choice but to fall into a deep slumber, one terrorized by the creature's implanted nightmares."

"So...she's not dead?"

"No, though if she stays in the fearstate for too long she will be. The brain can only handle a nightmare for so long before waking up. And if the body isn't warmed up before that, then it won't."

"Shit," Lumen said, holding her hands behind her head. She began to pace the floor. "We've got to go get her then. We've got to go down there and—"

"No," Parenti said. "No one leaves the rec room."

Lumen halted her pacing and spun around on Parenti. "Why the hell not?"

Parenti took a moment to gather his thoughts, to find the logic in them. He found it best to do so in times of stress. If he could find the logic in a situation, then he could construct a wall out of it. To protect himself, yes, but also to build toward a solution. After a moment had passed, he began laying the first brick.

"It's too dangerous. The Amygdalom is a mind reader. It knows our fears as well as we do, and as well as it knew Margo's. If we go down there, the chances that we end up just like her are more likely than anything."

Lumen's eyes were growing hotter every second. "So what? You just want to sit here and hide?"

"I want to sit here and *wait*," Parenti said, matching the edge in her voice with an edge of his own. "What's happening to Margo right now, it's happening slowly. The Amygdalom won't kill her until it's fed on all the fear she has, until it's *drained* her, and that process is long."

"How long?"

"As long as it can get." Parenti shrugged. "Depending on a person's fears, the Amygdalom could hypothetically feast for days, weeks even. Twenty-four hours is average among humans, however. Twenty-four hours before the mind breaks and the fearstate becomes fatal."

"So what exactly is your point?" Lumen asked, shaking her head. "You want to wait twenty-four hours to do something?"

"No," Parenti said, and he tapped twice on the keyboard before leaning back to reveal a new screen open on the corner computer. It showed the ship's ETA to Qlaus. "I want to wait thirteen."

He made another tap to show the time with seconds included. Thirteen hours, twenty-two minutes, four seconds and counting. "If we can hold out until we get to Qlaus, we can have HQ toxify the ship from the outside, kill the Amygdalom without risk to us and save Margo with time to spare."

The more he spoke, the more Parenti could visualize the wall rising around him. Built with logic, he knew that it was firm, that it would protect him, and the fact alone made him calm.

"So you just want to leave her out there until then?" Lumen asked, tone still ripe with disbelief.

"It's not ideal, I know, but it's our best option. The one that assures the highest possible chance of success while simultaneously taking the least risk." Parenti didn't like the sound of his words as they came out of his mouth, knew they must have sounded cold. But then, logic's job wasn't to be liked, but to be right. And so it often was cold.

"Thirteen hours," said Felix, and the look on his face was enough to scrape a painful chink in Parenti's wall. That was the thing about the cold, pain always hurt worse.

"Look," Parenti said, trying to reassure himself as much as the others. "These Amygdaloms, they're dangerous. To us on this ship and to the galaxy at large. I don't know how one got on the Phenomena, but the important thing is that it doesn't get anywhere else. If something like that were to get loose at a place like HQ, the result would be—"

"Chaos," Lumen said absently. Her arms were crossed tight against her chest, her eyes locked on the ground.

"Exactly. Which means we need to stay ready to comm it in when we get there; we need to stay alive. If not for ourselves then for Qlaus. It's the right thing to do," Parenti said, and he nudged his glasses up the bridge of his nose. "The logical thing."

Though it seemed for a moment like Lumen might protest, she ultimately relented, letting out a sigh before returning to her seat at the adjacent counter. Opening up her handheld, she just as soon closed it, opting to sit with her chin in her arms instead. Beside her, Felix looked even more anxious than usual.

Parenti did his best to ignore their expressions. Their emotions. So often the enemy of logic, Parenti tried as often as he could to prevent his own emotions from bleeding through, from interfering with harder facts. A lifelong effort, he'd become pretty good at suppressing them when needed. It was watching other people grapple with them that always gave him the most trouble.

Turning back to the computer, he focused his attention elsewhere, letting his emotions rest safely behind his fully constructed wall.

He got maybe five minutes before it all came tumbling down.

It started with a sound, a slight sound followed by an even slighter sensation. The halting of a previously unperceived humming and a similarly unperceived momentum. The latter caused Parenti to shift maybe half an inch where he sat, and a second later the intercom was playing.

"Ship temperature 40 degrees. Engines disengaged for power conservation."

"No," Parenti breathed.

Lumen was up again. "What now?"

Parenti was already bent over the keyboard. "That's not good," he said, tapping fast, trying desperately to find the mistake, to find out where the computer had gone wrong, only he couldn't. His own check coincided with what the intercom had just announced. The ship's temperature was at 40 degrees, and the engines had stopped because of it. "That's *not* good."

"What's not good?" asked Lumen.

"The engines..." Parenti said, continuing to stare at the computer screen. "They've stopped, gone into power conservation mode in response to the dropping temperature."

"Why does it keep dropping?"

"It's the Amygdalom," he said, turning to face her. "Its biology is such that it lowers the temperature all around it. Bad news for a heat-powered ship like the Phenomena 7. I'd suspected it had something to do with the cameras dropping, but to cause the engines to turn off...I wouldn't have thought it possible."

Lumen was shaking her head. "So what does that mean for us? I mean, without the engines we're stuck, right?"

"And worse I'm afraid. The engines are significant heat producers while they're running. Without them, the ship is entirely dependent on the furnace for heat. Of course, this would be fine except for the fact that there's something actively lowering the temperature on the ship."

"Meaning?"

"Meaning it's only a matter of time before the cold trumps the heat. And when that happens, the engines aren't the only thing that will stop working. The lights will likely go first, followed by the security and gravity locks, the ship's computer, and finally, the oxygen itself." Parenti returned his gaze to Lumen from where it had fallen. "Without those engines running, we're as good as dead."

With these last words, Parenti was reminded of the downside of logical thinking. Just like you could use logic to support you, to build a wall around yourself and be defended from the chaos beyond, you could just as easily do the opposite, build a tomb for yourself and lock the chaos inside.

"So let's turn the engines back on," Lumen said.

Parenti shook his head, falling further into that tomb every second. "We can't. As long as the Amygdalom is out there lowering the temperature, the engines won't leave power conservation mode."

"Okay, so let's kill that thing and *then* turn the engines back on."

Parenti's fall was suddenly halted. "What?"

Lumen raised her hands. "Listen, I know you said that it's dangerous, that if we have a choice we shouldn't even risk messing with it, but that's the thing. It's not looking like we *have* a choice. Not anymore."

Parenti blinked as he considered her logic, measured it against his own, and slowly worked his way up out of that tomb. She was right. This was the most logical choice now, their only choice, and had he not been so wrapped up in his own despair, he might have realized it himself. He kicked himself for not doing so. He'd let it happen, let his emotions get the best of him, cloud his logic.

He hated when that happened.

"You're right," he said, nodding slowly. "We don't." He continued to nod, continued until he felt himself come all the way up out of that tomb, stand on solid ground again.

Lumen seemed surprised at first by Parenti's agreement, but she quickly smiled. It was an easy smile, one not dictated by logic or fear or anything it seemed. Parenti found himself envious of it.

"So how do we do it? How do we beat the cold?"

Parenti's eyes went first to his density gun, and then to the rec room stove.

"With heat," he said, and with a new wall envisioned, he carefully laid the first brick.

***

It took Parenti about twenty minutes to construct the flamethrower. An impressive time, considering the meager tools he had to work with. But then, he'd been tinkering with the idea for months.

Lumen let out a whistle, grin wide above her lip rings. "Okay, now *that's* badass." She turned to Felix, gave him a shove on the shoulder. "You see that, Felix?"

Though he flinched beneath the shove, the young man was grinning too. "Badass," he agreed.

Parenti met their grins with his own. "Now, to see if it's functional."

After a few more adjustments, Parenti slowly pulled down on the trigger of his modified density gun, watching as a gout of flame emerged from the elongated nozzle. Initially a hissing candlelight, more pressure on the trigger meant more volume, one Parenti increased until the flame was a ripping, two-foot column, roaring through the air and bathing the room in a red-yellow glow.

Lumen's grin had grown even wider. "Oh yeah, she's functional all right." Practically skipping around the edge of the counter, she presented her own density gun to him in both hands. "Sorry, Felix, but he's *gotta* do mine next."

Parenti lowered the flamethrower with a frown. "I'm afraid I can't."

At Lumen's glare, he motioned to the stove, to its top where one of the four burners now sat gutted and hollow. "The stove only has so much propane. Enough for one flamethrower at best. To make another and divide the fuel in half would be to render both useless.

"Besides," he said, turning his eyes to the doors, "I'm going alone."

"Um...like hell you are," Lumen said, taking a step between the door and him. Felix too, took a step in protest, though he said nothing.

"I'm afraid I must," Parenti said. "I'm sorry, but it's too dangerous."

"Which is exactly why we *should* go," Lumen said, glaring. "So we can't all have flamethrowers. Fine." She held up her density gun, let it spin on her finger. "I'm willing to bet that isn't the only way of hurting this thing."

Felix nodded along with her. "Better odds," he said, taking another step forward.

Parenti felt a smile pull at his lips. The kid was braver than he looked. They both were. He let it fall all the same.

"It's not that simple," he said, shaking his head. "The Amygdalom, it's a magician, an illusionist. It makes you see your deepest fears, yes, but it can cast other veils too. Can confuse a battlefield quicker than anything, and the more people present, the greater the risk."

He raised a hand in front of him, pointed a finger gun at the door. "One minute you think you're shooting the Amygdalom, the monster, whatever thing you fear most." He moved his arm to the side, swung it until the finger gun pointed at Lumen. "Only for the illusion to fade and reality to show you something completely different." He let his arm fall.

"I've read reports about it. Horror stories. A single soldier gunning down his entire platoon, thinking they were monsters or whatever, only for the illusion to fade and the Amygdalom to feast on a brand-new fear materialized." Parenti shook his head. "I don't want to risk that. Sending one person eliminates the risk, and so it's the right thing to do." He nodded to them and to himself. "The logical thing."

Lumen still wasn't convinced. "So what? You expect us to just sit here with our thumbs up our asses?"

"Quite the opposite," Parenti said, tapping at the communicator on his belt. He set it to the hands-free setting, making it so that a proximity echo immediately began to sound over Lumen's and Felix's receivers. "You two will be my tether," he explained, and his words now came from each of their communicators with a static hiss. "If the Amygdalom manages to scare me, if at any point I confuse illusion with reality, the two of you will remind me." He tapped lightly on the holstered device. "The two of you will pull me back in."

Lumen was still shaking her head. "I don't know about this, Parenti—" She brought her hands over her ears as a loud echo screeched out over their receivers. "Can you shut that thing off?"

Parenti nodded that he could. With the press of a button, he opened the back double doors. He'd been inching his way toward them ever since completing the flamethrower, simultaneously nodding toward the front as if that were his intended exit. Lumen and Felix having positioned themselves in front of the latter, it left the former wide open. Taking a backwards step now through the silver threshold, he nodded at them.

"See you on the other side," he said, and with a tap on the control panel, he shut the doors in front of him.

Seconds later, he heard movement on the other side, pings on the control panel as Lumen no doubt attempted to open the doors from within.

"Don't bother," Parenti said. "They're locked."

"You can't lock the rec room doors, Parenti," Lumen snapped.

"No, but you can hack them."

"What—?" Through his communicator, Parenti heard the buzzing that denoted an incorrect entry on the control panel's keypad. Through the door, he heard a slam as well as some choice words.

"I'm sorry, but it's for your safety—"

More choice words through the door interrupted him. Parenti waited until they had subsided.

"I'm sorry, but what's done is done. I'm going to go on now. Can I count on the two of you to tether me?"

A moment passed in silence.

"Lumen, Felix, are you there?"

"I'm here," came Felix's voice through the static.

"And Lumen?"

"She's, um...she's—"

"I'm here, you pretentious asshole," she said.

Parenti nodded. "I deserved that."

"Damn right you did. And if you die out there, it'll be your own damn fault."

Parenti hesitated. "I—"

"So do us all a favor and don't die, okay?"

Parenti felt himself smiling. "I wouldn't dream of it."

Lumen's sigh yawned out over the radio. "For a smart guy, that dude can be a real dumbass."

"Er, Lumen? Your receiver is still on."

"I know."

Parenti nodded again. "Right."

He turned to the hallway stretched out before him, looked down at the flamethrower in his hands. At a tug of the trigger, a small flame materialized at its front. "All right," he said with a nod. "I'm moving out."

***

"How's it look out there?"

"Clear," Parenti said. At least the first two hallways had been. He rounded the third and found the same. "Still no feed on the cameras?"

"No," Lumen said after a moment. "All black."

Parenti nodded to himself. He'd figured as much. It seemed he'd be traveling blind. He rounded a corner and was met with yet another empty hallway. It was a big ship, the Phenomena 7, big enough that just finding the thing might prove a challenge in itself. But find it he would. With every step bringing him inexorably closer, it was only a matter of when.

Upon rounding the next corner, Parenti found himself in the engineering bay. It, much like the hallways before it, was empty. He kept on.

"What if you can't find it?" Lumen asked, her voice reverberating loudly in the empty space. Parenti found himself glad to hear it. There was a silence to the ship without its engines on that he'd never heard before, a silence that he wasn't sure he liked.

"I'll find it."

"It won't try to hide from you?"

"It has no reason to. Between the two of us, it has the advantage."

"That's reassuring."

"It's just the facts. Advantage doesn't always mean victory."

"Let's hope you're right. See anything yet?"

"No," Parenti said, rounding the next corner. He was on a new floor now, one level above the cargo bay and the lower quadrants. "But I can feel it."

"You what?"

"The cold," he clarified. He'd felt it as soon as he'd left the rec room, a chill that had slowly grown the farther he'd gone. Slowly deepened.

It was intense now. It bit at his exposed parts, made his nose run, sent goosebumps prickling up the back of his neck. Had it not been for his exosuit, he knew he'd be freezing, all skin shivers and teeth chatters. He wondered how much bodily excess was, at this very moment, being recycled to keep him insulated. The thought alone was enough to send an entirely new chill up his spine, the likes of which convinced him to stop thinking about it. He could tell now why the ship's engine had stopped. He wondered now how long it would be before his own engine did the same.

"What's the ship's internal temperature at now?" he asked.

"Looks like...36."

Parenti shook his head. 36. Four more degrees and it would be freezing. He knew the ship's oxygen system could operate at below freezing temperatures, but he couldn't remember its exact limit. Nor could he remember at what temperature the ship's other vital operations ceased function. Whatever the numbers, they had to be getting close. He was about to ask Lumen to check the computer when a sound ahead made him freeze.

The sound, unmissable in the silence of the ship, was a wet one. A sharp squelch followed by a softer pull, like something was being dragged across the floor. Something big.

"I found it," Parenti said, stopping dead. He could hear a gurgling now.

"You see it?" Lumen's voice came loud over the speaker.

"No," he said, eyeing the corner ahead of him. Somewhere beyond it, that squelch-drag neared ever closer. "But I can hear it." He wrinkled his nose, felt a heave in his stomach. "I can *smell* it."

"Well where is it? Where are you?"

"The East—" Parenti started, but was interrupted by another heave, all the way up his throat this time. He shuddered as he swallowed it back down. He didn't do well with bad smells. And this one was horrible.

He made a move to modify his exosuit, make the microfibers stretch over his face like a mask, but stopped short. *It's not real*, he reminded himself. The smell was nothing but an illusion, a trick created by the Amygdalom to fool his senses, to scare him. Convincing though it was, he knew activating his mask would only succeed in making it more so, would only play further into the Amygdalom's game. And Parenti had had enough games for one day.

"I'm in the East Second hallway," he said, steadying himself.

"And the thing?"

"The hallway adjacent. It's rounding the corner now...I—I can see it."

"What does it look like?"

"It's...it's..."

It was a mound. Of what substance Parenti could not be sure, though its sickly appearance did well to fill his mind with the worst assumptions. It was a brown thing mostly, though there were other colors there too. Dark blacks and sour yellows. Blood reds and flaming whites. It was a large thing, much larger than Parenti. It filled the entire width of the hallway with its horrible mass, and much of the height too. That he'd heard it dragging itself through the hallway now seemed understandable, if not still impossible. Nothing this big should have been able to move in the way this thing did. It seemed against the rules of physics if not nature itself.

But drag itself it did, toward Parenti like a great big slug. An amalgam of filth.

"What, Parenti? What is it?"

Parenti was forced to take a step back. "I don't...I don't know," he said, and his words sounded different than they usually did. Higher-pitched. More strained. He wondered if it was because of what he was doing with his throat, because of how he was still trying to keep the heaving down.

Lumen's voice came over the speaker again, clearer than before, adamant. "Okay, listen to me, Parenti, whatever you're seeing down there, it's not real. It's just the fearnapper playing tricks like you told us. Casting illusions."

Parenti stopped his retreat.

She was right. All the things he was seeing, all the things he was *smelling*, they were all just things in his head. Fears in his head. Ones the Amygdalom had fished out and put on a horrifying display in front of him, but that didn't make them real.

"An illusion," he said, and he looked down at the flamethrower. Unlike the monster before him, that was real. He squeezed it tighter as he stepped forward. "Just an illusion."

"Damn right," Lumen said. "Now look at that thing for what it really is."

Parenti pushed his glasses up the bridge of his nose. "Right."

It was harder than he expected, seeing through the veil. The smell of it creeping up his nostrils alone was enough to break his concentration, but eventually he managed, eventually he began to break through.

"It's working!" he exclaimed, raising the flamethrower. "I'm starting to see—"

His words were cut off by a wet pop. A part of the mound had ruptured then, had burst open like a great pimple and sent a long gout of discharge squirting out from within. It hit Parenti with a semi-solid smack, coating his face, blacking out his lenses.

"What do you see now?" came a voice through the darkness.

Parenti was immediately doubled over, coughing, spitting at the foul substance which now covered his lips, praying to God that he hadn't gotten any in his mouth. He pulled his glasses off and wiped the lenses clean, cringing all the time for the feel of the stuff on his fingers. It was warm.

"Parenti!" called Lumen from his waist. "What's happening?"

"It—it—it...it *spit* on me!" Parenti said, knowing he was yelling and not caring. The stuff had gotten all over his face. His *face*.

"No it didn't, Parenti!" Lumen yelled back. "Remember, it's just an illusion! An illusi—"

Lumen's words were cut off by another gout of discharge, this one catching Parenti's torso. It caked his communicator in the thick pus, muffling Lumen's words to a low vibration.

"No!" Parenti screamed, immediately working the gunk out of the speaker with his fingers, though he only managed a few seconds before the act overwhelmed him. It was just too gross.

He went to wipe what little he'd gotten on his fingers on his pant leg and in doing so got some on his forearm which in turn dripped down onto his boot too. "Damn it!" he cried, clutching his hands to his head in frustration, though that only served to get more in his hair, on the top of his ear, down the back of his neck. Soon he was retching again. The smell of it was just too strong, the warmth of it too suffocating. He must not have gotten it all when he'd wiped down his glasses, for he could feel a bit on the rims of his lenses, stinging his eyes with its stink. He felt tears welling up.

"What's wrong, Parenti?" asked the mound, sliding toward him, oozing.

Hearing his name served to snap Parenti back to reality, slow down his spiral. Suddenly, a bit of that logic was back in the forefront. Only a bit, but it was enough for him to latch on to, enough for him to steady himself. He did so slowly, raising himself straight again to face the monster before him. It had grown a crooked slit in its front, a diagonal mouth of sorts. It flapped open in a grin as it spoke.

"Something in your eye?"

Another part of it suddenly burst, sending a hot shower forward, speckling Parenti's glasses with a red-yellow residue. Parenti did not waver.

"You're not real," he said through gritted teeth.

"No?" said the mound, and the ground beneath it began to change color, began to fill with a thick, dark red secretion. It flowed quickly to Parenti, surrounded his boots, submerged him to the toe and kept rising.

"No," he said, feeling the liquid rise beneath him, watching the pus drip down his lenses. He did his best to ignore both. He could still feel the vibration of Lumen's voice through his communicator, and though he could no longer make out her words, he knew what they must have said. He said them to himself instead.

"All of this...it's just an illusion."

He raised the flamethrower again, stared hard at the monster before him, visualized what it truly looked like. He'd seen it before in the camera feed. Logic said it wouldn't be hard to recreate the image. But then a bit of that pus ran to the edge of his lens, dripped down onto his upper lip and curled its way into his mouth.

Suddenly, all logic was out the window.

This time it was more than just a heave. Parenti puked down the front of his exosuit, kicking himself all the while. He knew it wasn't real, he *knew* that. And yet, he also knew what that bit of discharge had felt like on his tongue, and its putrid taste was enough to render it a real of its own.

"Just an illusion?" taunted the Amygdalom, sliding forward. *"Are you sure?"*

Parenti thrust the flamethrower forward. "Stay back!" he screamed. He made an attempt to straighten himself, to look at the Amygdalom and see it for what it truly was, but all he could see was the mound.

"Your friends tried that too, you know," it hissed, skin bubbling as it spoke. *"Tried to face their fears and see the real me."* As it lurched forward, a chunk of itself fell off at the side, hit the now flooded floor with a bloody splash. *"Not even they could do it, and they were much braver than you."*

"Shut up!" Parenti screamed, though he knew it was right. Shaking with a combination of fear and cold, he forced himself to keep looking, to keep trying to see it. "I don't need to be as brave as them," he said, pushing his glasses up. "I know what you are, and I know how to stop you."

He pulled the trigger then, lit up the hallway with flame. He watched as a ball of it engulfed the mound, and kept watching as the fire scorched it from the outside in. He must have held the trigger for ten seconds in all, until even in the cold he couldn't stand the peripheral lick of the blaze. He released the trigger with a satisfying thought, one founded, as most satisfying thoughts were, in logic. With enough heat, anything could be destroyed.

Anything, it seemed, but the Amygdalom.

"No," Parenti breathed, blinking in disbelief, though his eyes did not deceive him.

The mound was still there, was still intact, and was, as it had been from the start, still dragging itself toward him.

"No!" Parenti screamed, and he pulled the trigger again, filled the hall with another column of fire. This one lasted only a second before the flamethrower was knocked from his hands.

"Ah, ah, ah," sang the Amygdalom. *"Can't you tell it's too late for that?"* It had changed shape now, had grown a collection of tendrils, each one a long, slithering leech.

Parenti made a lunge for the flamethrower but the tendrils caught him before he could reach it. They wrapped themselves over him, coiling like snakes around his wrists, his ankles, his torso, and his neck.

"No!" Parenti screamed, bucking against them, calling out in both rage and fear. "You can't do this! I know what you are! I know what *mmphh—*"

The tendrils around his throat had grown, had risen to cover his mouth.

"Know, know, know, know, know. You know so much, Parenti. Have you ever thought that maybe that's the problem?"

All the tendrils were growing now, were lengthening to expand over Parenti's entire body. To wrap him in a cocoon.

"There's a safety in ignorance, you know. A courage inherent to naivety. What you don't know can't hurt you, right? But then, what if you do *know? What if you know too much?"*

Parenti was crying now, he felt so gross. He couldn't see anything, the tendrils having tightened over his eyes. He couldn't move, though he tried to speak, a muffled whimper beneath the mound.

"What was that?" it said, and it opened its tendrils enough around Parenti's face for him to see out, enough for him to breathe.

"You're...not...*real*," he choked.

The Amygdalom only smiled its long, diagonal smile.

"Don't you get it yet?" it said, and it drew Parenti close, so close that he could see the inside of its mouth now, could see the darkness which lay within. Could smell it. *"Don't you understand?"* It tightened its grip on him, enough to squeeze out the air in his lungs, enough to kill him, though it didn't.

With the small black eyes of its true self peeking through the flesh of the mound, it said, *"I'm as real as you make me."*

Parenti succumbed then. To the cold, his body going numb, the world going blue. And to the fear, his mind turning over, and that blue world turning black. As he faded, all his senses fading with him, his smell stayed. His smell and that horrible stench to go with it. That stench of filth.

That stench of the mound.

Lumen

L umen was in the dark. Had been for a while now. She
found there were few things more agonizing.

"Parenti!" she called into the communicator. "Parenti, do
you copy?" she asked for the fiftieth time. She released the
trigger, listened, for the fiftieth time, to the low hiss of static
from the radio speaker, and heard, for the fiftieth time, no
response.

"God damn it!" she yelled, throwing the receiver to the
ground. It being connected by a coiled cord to the communicator still attached to her waist, it didn't go far, though the
impact of it on the floor made Felix jump all the same.

Without bothering to pick it up, she strode to the other
side of the rec room, to where the stove sat, the receiver
dragging along behind her all the way.

Without much of a plan, she began to disassemble one of
the remaining stove tops, trying to recall how Parenti had
done it before. She got to what she thought she remembered
as the third step before something stumped her, and she
found herself trying to detach a fixture that wouldn't budge.

She had just turned around to try pressing it from a new angle when she caught Felix looking at her from across the room, just staring at her through those dark dreads of his.

"What?" she said, coming off nastier than she'd meant.

He shook his head, quickly looked somewhere else.

"You remember how he made that flamethrower?" she said, motioning to the stove.

Another shake of the head. "Too fast."

Lumen nodded. Too fast was right. She'd played her fair share of games with crafting systems, those games where you'd find some items in one level and craft them together to get through the next. A novel mechanic, though one she'd always kind of resented. It was just too fast. Too *gamey*. In games like that, your character could turn a pile of junk into the most useful tool ever, and they could do it in a matter of seconds. That wasn't realistic. Nobody could actually do that.

But then there was Parenti.

The dude was something else. Easily the smartest person she'd ever met, it made the fact that he'd made such a stupid decision all the more infuriating. Abandoning her half-dis-assembled stove top with a groan, she turned to the next Parenti-project, receiver still trailing behind her like a dog on a leash.

Though she'd tried the control panel already, she tried it again, punching in the open code to see if it might work now. It didn't. She tried a couple more times, just to see if it might work *then*, but it was useless. Unless she could find a way to override it, Parenti's hack was here to stay.

Tepidly, she opened the software configurations and almost immediately accepted defeat. The lines of code might as well have been another language. Technically, they were. And Lumen had never been fluent. Still she tried, punching in commands and hoping for the best. When, after a few minutes, it became clear that she was only making things worse, she let her forehead slam against the screen in defeat.

"Can I try?" Felix's voice came from behind her.

"Be my guest," she said, stepping back. "That asshole hacked it good. I don't know if we'll—"

She was interrupted by an electronic ding, one followed by a color change on the control panel from red to green. A second later, the screen was out of the configurations and back to the keypad. Felix side-stepped away, hands shoved deep in his pockets. Keeping his eyes on the ground, he nodded toward the door. "It should work now."

"What, you fixed it?" Lumen said, narrowing her eyes at the screen.

Felix nodded.

"How?"

"Well um, the ship's code, it's...well it's just like this game I play—"

"*Integer Infintenima?*"

Felix looked up then, wide eyes telling Lumen she'd guessed right.

She nodded. "I don't play it, more into action-adventure than puzzle-strategy, but I've seen it. Couple guys at my old job were obsessed with it. Could never shut up about the newest levels." She narrowed her eyes at Felix, looked him up and down. "Never pegged you as a gamer."

He only shrugged in reply.

Lumen smiled. Felix was a weird kid. Like that song in your playlist that you can never really figure out the words to, but you like it, so you sing along anyway.

The whole crew was like that in a way. Each member their own song. Having only been on the job for a few months together, she didn't know all the words yet, but she knew she liked them, and that was enough.

She eyed the screen again, came back to Felix. "You up for a boss fight?"

Felix's eyes met hers, and the way they stared at her from behind his dreads, unwavering, she could tell he was.

She nodded. "Good, 'cause I'm gonna need you out there. We're gonna need *each other*. None of this going alone bull-shit, yeah? I don't care what Parenti says. I feel better with somebody having my back. You got mine?"

Felix nodded.

"Good. I've got yours." She eyed his waistband, noticed an absence. "You got a density gun?"

He shook his head.

Lumen tossed hers to him. "Here."

He caught it at his chest, regarding it and then her with confusion.

"Don't worry," she said, answering his silent question. "I'm banking on that flamethrower still being down there," She then turned to one of the roller chairs and lifted it up off the floor. It was heavy, with thick cushions and a long steel bar running along the bottom for support. She raised it above her head and slammed it to the ground. From the wreckage, she was able to pry that bar loose. She tapped it against her palm a few times to check the weight and found that it, too, was heavy. "This should do."

"Melee." Felix grinned.

Lumen grinned back.

Above, the intercom jingled with another message.

"Ship temperature 32 degrees, critical systems will soon disengage."

Lumen looked up at the blue announcement light, frowning as the electronic script slid silently across the text box. *Time trial*, she thought. Those had always been her least favorite levels.

"We've gotta go," she said, stepping to the doors. She turned to Felix. "You ready?"

Felix gave a nod, punched the code into the keypad. Before them, the silver double doors opened, and a blast of cold washed over them from the hall beyond.

Lumen grit her teeth against the chill, pulled the zipper on her exosuit all the way to the collar. "All right," she said, gripping the bar a little tighter. "Let's do this."

***

The cold, palpable the minute they'd left the rec room, only got worse as they went.

It bit the worst at Lumen's face and hands, the places left exposed by her exosuit, and so she covered them. It still surprised her how fast the nanonylon went. Without a spiky mohawk to navigate around, the microfibers could encapsulate her much quicker.

Though ideal for the situation, it still made her sad. She'd rocked the mohawk for years. Since *Total Terraform II* had come out, and now *Total Terraform V* was right around the corner. Having gotten it for Layla, the main character of TTII back on her 21st birthday, she'd just recently gotten rid of it for her 26th. It wasn't that she didn't like Layla anymore, or even Total Terraform, but rather that she had been ready for a change. And a drastic one at that. Since the fourth grade, she'd modeled her hairstyle after video game characters, ever since she'd first seen Mona from *Amberdom* and insisted she have braids just like her. After that it had been Dominique from *Super Sugar Space Pop*, Tully from *Death Mavericks*, and so on and so forth until she'd gotten to Layla. Her newest do was the odd one out. A simple buzz and bleach, it was the first time in years she hadn't based the style off a video game character. It was the first time in years she'd just been her.

She was happy with the new style, though she still missed the mohawk from time to time. Missed the punkiness of it, missed the way people's eyes would move up as they looked at her, as if it was the tallest thing in the world, missed what it meant. Right now, she missed the extra warmth of it too. For even that lone strip of hair was better to face the cold with than none at all.

And it was cold as hell.

It wasn't hard to tell when they were closing in on it, the Amygdalom. The cold gave it away. Seeing their breath steam out more and more in front of them, spying the thin layer of frost grow steadily thicker over the cabin walls, it was like a reversed version of that old hot-cold searching game. For while Lumen and Felix may have been closing in on their target, they certainly weren't getting any warmer.

It was upon entering the engineering bay, a large, circular room toward the center of the ship that they finally saw it. It stood motionless at the opposite end of the room, standing there like it had been waiting for them. Lumen supposed it had.

She wasn't sure what she'd been expecting, had only been able to guess at what might truly be her deepest fear, but of all her theories, none had been this. The Amygdalom took the form of a skeleton. Some seven or eight feet tall, it towered over her and Felix, staring at them with glowing green eyes, smiling at them with an eternal grin. It held a sword in one hand, and a shield in the other, both of an olden make which matched the rest of its wares. Adorned in fur-ridden armor, a long leather kilt, and a steel helmet with two curling horns of bone, the getup was unmistakable. This was a Viking. A skeletal Viking, as the long brown beard which hung from its skinless cheekbones indicated. One Lumen knew well.

This was Skelevik.

Skelevik was a boss from *Nightmarish,* and he was the very worst one. Not only was he notoriously hard to beat, but his difficulty was amplified by a devastating mechanic: if you died to Skelevik, your game would be reset.

It didn't matter if you'd saved before, didn't matter if you'd played for a hundred hours already, if you died to Skelevik, if you saw his gray, grinning face in your game over screen, that meant it was truly over. Your progress would be wiped, your data reset, and you'd have to start the entire game over from the beginning. A brutal consequence, it was balanced only by the alternative. If you beat Skelevik, you acquired Skullman's Cap, a significant stat booster, and an item needed in order to unlock the game's true ending.

The quasi-final boss of the game, Skelevik's dungeon is open to players from the very beginning, meaning you can challenge him as soon as you beat the tutorial if you want. However, due to his stats, he's nearly impossible to beat at such a low level. The stronger you get, leveling up by progressing the story and defeating other bosses, the better your chances become for defeating him, but the more you have to lose for failing too. The end result was a genius gameplay mechanic. A scary one.

Lumen had beaten Skelevik before. Twice actually. Once for herself, and once for a friend who was too nervous to do it on their own. She'd beaten him before, but that didn't make him any less scary. It never did. Fighting Skelevik meant taking a chance, meant putting everything on the line. Lumen had done it before though, and so she knew she could do it again.

She turned to Felix, staring wide-eyed beside her. She didn't know what he was seeing, but she guessed it wasn't Skelevik. Judging by the look on his face, she guessed it was something much, much worse.

She nudged his shoulder with the chair bar.

"Hey, remember, not real."

He nodded to her, closed his eyes for a second before turning back to it. When he opened them again, the fear was gone. Lumen watched him draw her density gun from his waist.

"All right, Amygda-lame!" she shouted, drawing her own weapon, giving the bar a spin before resting it on her shoulder. It was the emote her *Nightmarish* character did before every boss battle, and she'd recreated it perfectly. She felt a grin pulling at her lips as she began her approach, and she wasn't sure if it was out of fear or excitement. Probably it was both. "Bring it on!" she said, and ran forward.

One thing to know about Skelevik, he always, *always* opens with an overhead swing. Lumen had seen it a million times, and she'd dodged it almost just as many. She did so this time and felt that grin pulling wider as she remembered something Parenti had said earlier. If the Amygdalom was reading her mind, using her memories of Skelevik to scare her, then was it also using her memories of Skelevik's moveset? A moveset she just so happened to have memorized?

It seemed so.

As he came at her again, this time with a low sweep as familiar as the overhead swing, Lumen evaded and—just like she always did in-game—perfect countered, bashing Skelevik in the face with a two-handed swing of her bar.

"Eat it!" she screamed, basking in the thrill of it. *Nightmarish* being a third-person game, it was surreal to watch the attack from a first-person perspective.

That was not the only difference.

In-game, a perfect counter triggered a mini cinematic, one that differed depending on which boss you were fighting. For Skelevik, it was his helmet going askew, and him pushing it back into place before coming at you with a renewed vengeance. This being so far a faithful adaptation, the Amygdalom mimicked the animation, only it was joined by something new. Upon smashing the bar into its face, a dark blue mist seemed to have enveloped Skelevik's skull, one that sank in on itself before regaining solidity, before changing back into that which it sought to represent. Once Skelevik had returned, he only grimaced, raised a great bony foot and thrust it into Lumen's chest, knocking her back.

The attack caught Lumen off-guard. Skelevik didn't kick.

As she recovered from the blow some feet away, Lumen made a mental note. It seemed the Amygdalom was throwing some of its own moves in, making it so that Skelevik's wasn't the only moveset she'd have to watch out for.

Pushing herself back to her feet, she saw that the Amygdalom had turned its attention to Felix, was approaching him under whatever guise frightened him most. Whatever it was, it wasn't so frightening that he couldn't fight back. Felix was shooting his density gun, only he kept missing. Lumen wondered too late if he'd ever fired one before.

Realizing she should have given him the bar instead, she hurled the thing in frustration, aimed it right at Skelevik.

"Hey Amygda-ass!" she yelled as it struck him in the back of the head, the impact once again knocking his helmet askew. She sprinted toward him. "We weren't done yet!"

Skelevik spun around instantly, hissing at her as he pushed his helmet back into place. Great jaw dropping low, he let go his most dangerous attack, a spewing vomit of screaming souls. Get hit with one of those in-game, and not only would half your health bar be depleted, but one of the souls would attach itself to you, slowly damaging you over time until you took a health potion. Not having a health potion, Lumen didn't want to find out what would happen in real life. Luckily, she didn't have to. She dodged his soul spew just like she had his other attacks, rolling out of the way and retrieving her bar in the process.

She spun it around again. "That's two now, skull-boy."

Skelevik was grimacing again. *"You're not scared,"* he said, and his voice sounded different than it did in game, sounded like that which he really was.

"What gave me away?" Lumen asked, giving the bar another spin.

"What really scares you?"

"Not you, ugly."

"Perhaps something else then..."

And he was changing again, face sinking into that smoky blue, morphing into something else. Lumen watched as, in a procession of undulating blue clouds, Skelevik disappeared, became but an outline of himself before becoming the outline of another. This one was not as tall as Skelevik, though it was a bit wider. And as the smoky blue-blacks gave way to more colors underneath, as this new thing slowly came into focus, Lumen realized that it was a thing she recognized. Another boss from *Nightmarish*.

Mumlord.

A not-so-humanoid mummy, with glowing black eyes and a huge, hulking upper body, the creature was more plant than man, and more dead than anything. From between the cracks in its haphazardly strung wrappings, the dark, leathery stems that made up its form could be spied, poking out in all the places they shouldn't, a collection of undead overgrowths. It was from these openings, the holes in its fingertips, the ever-yawning maw which was its mouth, that the creature attacked in a never-ending volley of dark vines, of biting teeth, and of black chrysanthemums.

Lumen knew Mumlord well, as well as she knew Skelevik. The plant monster wasn't as difficult as the skeletal Viking, though the mummified bastard had always given Lumen a hard time. Something about its moveset, about the timing she could never get quite right. About the way it gave her the creeps.

Mumlord smiled as if reading her thoughts, let go a violent cascade of rippling vines, the bulges of its body shrinking as their contents were depleted, the wrappings left behind sagging loose and limp.

Lumen dodged the attack, perfect countered, and brought the bar smashing down upon the mummy's head. "Three," she counted off.

Mumlord may have given her the creeps, but she'd beaten it even more times than she'd beaten Skelevik.

"You're still not scared," hissed the Amygdalom, and it didn't even try to pass as Mumlord any longer, had already begun to envelop itself in that smoky blue. *"Why aren't you—"*

The Amygdalom was cut off then, was stumbling forward suddenly, one still fully-Mumlord hand going to the back of its only half-Mumlord head. It turned around, and in doing so gave Lumen a view of what had hit it. Felix stood some feet away, density gun held steady in his outstretched hands. It seemed he'd finally gotten a hit.

Lumen smiled at him, and he smiled back.

A second later he was being pummeled by vines.

"No!" Lumen screamed, running forward, bar arm prepared to throw, but it was already too late.

Upon reaching Felix, the wall of dark, chrysanthemum-ridden vines slammed into him, took him off his feet with the impact and carried him further, out the bay door and into the hallway where they slammed him again into the outer wall.

"I'll deal with you later," hissed the Amygdalom, quickly retracting its vines, leaving Felix to fall in a heap to the floor.

"Felix!" Lumen screamed, watching his limp body with horror.

She saw his eyes open, saw him start to bring himself back to his feet when the doors to the hall slid closed, cut him off from the bay. The Amygdalom smashed the control panel, prevented the doors from opening again, locked Felix out.

Locked Lumen in.

"Just you and me now," it whispered.

"You sure that's a good idea for you?" she said, gripping the bar tight. "I'm at three now, you know." And she was itching to make it more.

The Amygdalom studied her carefully. *"You do have something that scares you,"* it said. *"What is it?"*

It didn't look like Mumlord anymore, had reverted back to its amorphous mist, was steadily returning to its actual form, the one Lumen had seen on the camera feed. That thin blue body and huge round head. It didn't scare her.

"Isn't that your job?" she asked, drawing closer, readying for her next attack. "You tell me."

"There's something there...I just can't find it."

It was morphing again, was trying to at least. Quickly and incompletely, it shifted before her, a new form every second, each one hypothetically scary, though not to Lumen.

Not until the last.

"Ah," said the Amygdalom. *"Here it is."*

Its body was black now, completely so. Black in a way that was more than just black. Black in a way that was absence of light. Black in a way that was darkness. Lumen couldn't help but be unnerved by the sight of it. There was something terribly alien about that total blackness. And something terribly familiar.

"I see it now," it said, holding up a dark hand, and as it did the space all around it seemed to dim. *"It was so bright in here that I didn't even think. That* you *didn't even think. But now..."*

Lumen swung at him again, because she wanted to, but also to fight the rising feeling in her chest.

The Amygdalom caught it with a hand.

"Ah, ah, ah," it cooed. *"No more of that. You've lost now."*

"Like shit I have," Lumen said, swinging again, though this blow was caught too.

"Don't lie to yourself. I know you feel it as well as I do. Your fear...it's growing."

"I can't feel shit," she said, though she was swinging faster now, more desperately.

"No? Perhaps if I accelerate the process."

A blast of cold air suddenly engulfed her, seemed to come at her from all sides, but mostly from the Amygdalom. A second later, the intercom jingle was playing again, the emotionless voice of the computer following.

"Ship temperature 28 degrees. Lights disengaged for power conservation."

The overhead lights shut off then, plunged the bay and the entire ship into darkness. The Amygdalom, before a black void in a single place before her, was suddenly in all places, was suddenly everywhere.

Lumen felt her heart drop.

A second later she was diving forward, sweeping wide with the chair bar, hacking and slashing in the direction of the Amygdalom. She hit nothing.

"Over here," it whispered from her left, making her jump. She swiped in that direction but hit nothing.

"No, here," it hissed, this time to her right.

This one had been closer than the first, and she pounced at it, attacked the blind space before her with a vicious strike. When again she hit nothing, she turned around, swung at the space behind her, and then at the space beside that. She must have made seven swings in all, hitting nothing with any of them.

It was while she was catching her breath from this volley that the Amygdalom whispered right into her ear, made her scream.

"Here."

Swinging the bar around her as she jumped backwards, Lumen stuck her arms out wide, hunched over slightly, felt for walls where there were none. The bay around her suddenly seemed huge. Seemed infinite.

"Where are you?" she screamed.

"Isn't it obvious, Lumen?" asked the bodiless voice, beginning at a place some paces ahead of her. It ended as a cold breath on the back of her neck. *"I'm everywhere."*

Lumen swung hard on the turnaround, went right into the wall, hard enough to make her knuckles vibrate, to make the bar go flying out of her hands on the rebound.

She made a move for it and stopped, kept one hand on the wall she'd found behind her, not daring to lose it again, to become lost in the darkness. Even if it meant staying defenseless.

She swore at herself, pounded her bad fist on the wall, made it worse, ended up bringing both hands to her face. She covered her eyes with them at first. Then, because that was even more darkness, lowered them, held them on her head instead, clutched at the absence of mohawk.

"Are you scared yet?"

"No," she spat, hating that she couldn't even see it. That its voice seemed to come from everywhere and nowhere all at once. She tried to key into that hate, use it to overpower the fear, but it was slow to go.

"I'm not scared of you," she said, and to prove it to herself, she stepped away from the safety of the wall, immersed herself anchorless in the looming black. "You're just an illusion."

"That's the thing, though," cooed the Amygdalom. *"I'm not. Not this time."*

The sound of its voice was enough to make Lumen stumble, retreat back to the wall, just brush her fingers on it for a second, only it was no longer there.

The Amygdalom laughed. *"Well, maybe a little bit. You see, usually I have to start from scratch. Create something that exists nowhere but within the mind. Other times there is no need. Other times I need only enhance what is already there."*

All around her, the darkness seemed to deepen, to expand and become darker than it already was.

Lumen felt her breath hitching in her throat, tried to slow it by holding her breath, but only managed to make it quicker on the output. She tried to take her mind off it, distract herself somehow.

She thought—as she so often did—of video games. Of all the badass characters she'd ever played, of all the monsters they'd slain, of all the darknesses they'd wandered themselves...but it was no use.

There was never true darkness in video games. Even in horror games, where the fundamental design was to throw you into a dark level and send terrifying NPCs to stalk you through it, there was always some kind of light. A lantern to fill with oil, a flashlight to fill with batteries, something. Even if there wasn't, even if a game pulled out all the stops and submersed you totally in the throes of a blacked-out screen, there was always the glow of the console itself, the RGB pulse that assured you that, even in the darkness of your room, that you were all right, that it was just a game.

But Lumen wasn't in her room, this was not a game, and she felt far, far away from all right.

A cool breath on her cheek made her shriek, made her take off running. She got three steps before crashing into a wall. Her face lit up with pain as she stumbled back, wary to move, yet terrified to stand still.

Another breath made her lash out with her nails. She caught the flat of her wrist on the edge of something hard enough to send her nerves singing, her mouth swearing, her eyes tearing up. She ambled forward, heard a grumbling and doubled back. It seemed there were more things in the bay now than just her and the Amygdalom. Lumen could hear them, could *sense* them.

She couldn't see them.

She was on the floor now, crawling backwards to she didn't know where. Bumping her head good on another wall, she screamed in frustration, and in fear too. She felt like the bay had suddenly become much smaller, a cramped closet. She felt like it had also become much bigger, an endless expanse. She knew that the two were impossible, but she also knew that her thinking them, her fearing them, made them both so. When you can't see, anything is possible.

She felt the Amygdalom before her, felt its cold.

"What did you say you were at?" it hissed. *"Three?"*

Lumen put her hands over her ears first, then over her eyes, closed them tight, figured her own darkness was better than the one beyond. It almost was.

The Amygdalom pulled her hands down, wrapped its own around her throat. Inches away, it blew cool air over her face as it spoke.

"I'm at four."

The cold advanced then, and the darkness too. Lumen tried to close her eyes, but the Amygdalom held them open, kept her in the darkness, forced her to watch, unseeing, as she was overcome.

Felix

Everything was going wrong, and Felix knew it.

Why did everything always go wrong?

He was running east down the South Second hallway, the quickest way back to the engineering bay.

Or, would west have been quicker?

No. East was quickest, he was pretty sure. Either way he'd already committed, would need to keep going if he was going to get back to Lumen.

Back to the Amygdalom.

He did his best not to think about that part. His crewmate was in trouble. His *friend* was in trouble. All his friends were, and he needed to get back there and save them. Needed to—

He'd just rounded the East Second corner when the intercom jingled, plunged the ship into darkness. He stopped dead.

What now?

Keep going.

He resumed his run. The hallways were straight and empty enough to run through blind, though he slowed his pace a little. Wouldn't want to—

Something on the floor tripped him up, sent him tumbling down. He rubbed the forearm he'd fallen on, felt with his feet for the thing that he'd hit. It hadn't been very big.

I don't have time for this, he decided, standing back up, preparing to resume his run.

But what had it been?

Curiosity got the better of him.

He walked back until he stepped on it, picked it up and tried to feel it out in the darkness. It had a strange shape to it, though at least one half was familiar. He fit his fingers around the trigger of a gun. A density gun. He knew because he'd just been firing Lumen's, though he hadn't been hitting much. Got it one time though.

Do I fire?

He figured his aim wasn't all that good, and he figured the darkness didn't help.

Should anyone fire a weapon in the dark?

If it was the weapon Felix thought it was, then maybe. He squeezed the trigger, fired it.

Fired it.

The darkness before him was suddenly penetrated by a column of orange flame, one that came from the end of the flamethrower Felix was holding. And at the end of the column? Parenti, standing wide-eyed and frozen, a look of terror on his face.

Felix jumped back, released the trigger, and Parenti's face disappeared. He pulled it again, lighter this time, let the flame linger.

Parenti's face came back, though it hadn't moved. It couldn't. None of him could.

The Amygdalom got him, it froze him in the fearstate.

Felix looked down at the flamethrower in his hands.

Should I unfreeze him?

He pressed harder on the trigger, let the flames loom closer to Parenti. He could see them dancing in the lenses of his glasses. He released the trigger again.

Is that even how it works?

A second later he had lowered the flamethrower, had decided that he didn't know what he was doing, and that there was no time anyway.

"I'm sorry," he said as he stepped around him.

I'll come back, he promised.

But first he had to save Lumen.

And he was running again, using the flamethrower to light his path, to fight off the cold and the darkness. He thought of Lumen fighting too, and that made him run faster. He felt his communicator on his hip as he ran.

Should I call her?

No. She wouldn't be able to answer. Not if she was fighting the Amygdalom.

Not if it had gotten her too.

He shook his head of that thought quick, kept running, faster, *faster*.

The flamethrower proved a dangerous thing to run with. Pull the trigger too hard and you risked spewing out too much, risked catching the backlash. Don't pull hard enough and you risked having no light at all, risked running in the dark, risked running into monsters. Felix found a happy medium. He'd squeeze it every three seconds or so, let off one big red puff before letting it die again, repeat the process once it had all gone black. The result was a kind of strobing hallway, like one of those old film reels, a new picture every few moments, each one interspersed with black.

He turned a corner during one of the puffs, saw the open door of the engineering bay at the other end. He ran faster. The second puff put him halfway to it, as well as a vague silhouette of something within.

Lumen.

Was she moving?

The flame died out before he could tell. He kept running.

The third puff brought him into the room, brought him before her.

Brought him before his fears.

Lumen stood impossibly still, as still as Parenti had, a similar look of terror etched into her pretty face.

No.

The flame died out, and because he couldn't believe it, Felix lit it again, shined its light on Lumen, made it make sure she was gone. She was.

They all were.

Felix let the trigger go, backpedaled in the darkness, felt the world collapsing around him.

No.

He thought of them: Casper, Margo, Parenti, Lumen. Thought of all the things they'd said to him, all the things he'd said to them. And all the things he hadn't.

They're all gone?

He thought of all the time he'd spent with them, of all the things he'd wanted to say but hadn't. And why? Because he was afraid he'd say the wrong thing? Because he was afraid he already had?

No, no, no.

It all seemed like a waste now. Wasted time, wasted opportunities, wasted fears. It was all so stupid. He was so stupid. So long he'd spent agonizing over things that didn't matter. Now none of it mattered.

Now they're all dead.

No, he thought, shaking his head. *They're not dead. Not yet. I can still do something. I can still save them.*

"No you can't."

A terrible voice from the other side of the room. *Its* terrible voice.

Felix spun with the flamethrower, managed to capture it in his light. Just a bit, though even that much was enough to send his hairs standing. The Amygdalom had embodied a humanoid form. Tall and muscular, with pale skin and long leathery wings. It smiled at Felix under piercing black eyes, beamed at him with a pair of long white fangs.

"I was hoping I'd get to you last."

Felix stepped forward, hoping to illuminate it further, however unsettling, to burn it. The Amygdalom was quicker though. It slunk easily back into the shadows, became one with them, *was* one with them, maybe. When again he heard its voice, it came from behind him.

"You're the special one."

Felix spun again, got a glimpse of it before it disappeared, saw mad red eyes and a dark gray pelt. A long snout like some kind of animal. Like some kind of wolf.

"Most people have something. One thing that really scares them."

From his left this time. Felix got his light on it in time to see the bulbous shape of a great worm-thing, its back half slithering off into the darkness.

"You though, you're different."

From his right then, and Felix felt he'd locked the pattern down, enough to spin around preemptively, get his light on it quicker than he had yet, see the Amygdalom in its entirety.

And see it he did.

It didn't turn away this time, flee back into the darkness. It only stood, staring back at him. Testing him. Scaring him.

It had taken the form of a robot this time, some metal-headed killing machine, a drill for one hand and a pair of sharp pincers for the other, though it didn't stay long. Morphing in a smoky blue mist before his eyes, Felix watched as the robot disappeared, reformed into a witch, all rotting skin and low, mumbling incantations. From the witch it went to a slime, and from the slime to a giant, disembodied eye.

One by one they came like this, an onslaught of morphing assailants, each one as terrifying as the last, if not worse.

"You're not scared of just one thing," the Amygdalom said, morphing into an undead version of Felix's mother. *"Or even a few things."* It went from an undead version of his mother to an undead version of Felix himself, slid a knife across its throat and spoke to him with its head dangling off the side of its neck. *His* neck.

"You're scared of everything.*"*

Felix closed his eyes. He couldn't bear to look anymore. Couldn't risk it. The Amygdalom was right. He *was* scared of everything.

"It's why I chose this ship," it said, and footsteps on the floor told Felix it was approaching. He kept his eyes shut.

"It had been a long time since I'd sensed so much fear in one place. And all of it cooped up in this little ship. In your little head."

The Amygdalom stepped closer and Felix fought back a shudder, still not opening his eyes.

"One whiff and I knew I had to find you. Of course, your friends were fun, but they were just a means to an end. A means to you."

Felix could feel the Amygdalom now, could tell by the cold that it was right in front of him. He opened his eyes, was met by his own dead, grinning face.

That's not me.

It wasn't. And it was upon that fact that he based the rest of his efforts, upon that fact that he made himself see through the illusion. Made himself see the Amygdalom as it truly was.

The change happened in seconds. With a familiar puff of blue smoke, Felix watched his doppelganger's face change, watched it expand and eventually disappear. What replaced it was the Amygdalom. Its light blue limbs were much thinner than Felix's, its round head much bigger. It looked down at itself and then to Felix, its small black eyes wide.

"You're not—" it said, taking a step back. It steadied itself, looked down at him accusingly. *"You're supposed to be afraid."*

Felix only nodded.

"That's the thing about being scared of everything," he said, raising the flamethrower. "You learn to be brave all the time."

The Amygdalom tried to jump away, tried to retreat back into the shadows, but it was too late. It had gotten too close, had fallen right into Felix's trap.

With the flick of a finger, Felix pulled the trigger and torched the blue bastard black.

Epilogue

Despite having two blankets wrapped around her, the ship's furnace to her back and a space heater Parenti had modified to her front, Margo felt colder than she ever had.

Parenti said it was only natural, that because she'd been in the fearstate the longest, that it would take her body the longest to recuperate. It made sense, but that didn't mean she had to like it.

Margo had been in the fearstate a total of 55 minutes compared to Parenti's 30 and Lumen's 15, a fact that likely explained why the two of them had stopped their shivering long before her. Though she thought she saw Parenti's teeth still chattering a bit.

55 minutes.

At first she hadn't believed them, when they'd told her, had insisted that she'd been gone longer...that she had to have been. That how could she have been this cold otherwise?

The fearstate, that place she'd gone, that place the Amygdalom had *taken* her, she felt like she'd been there for much longer than 55 minutes. An entire night felt more accurate, hours spent in constant terror, chased by Dresserdoc the clown through a feverish carnival. A never-ending nightmare.

She shuddered to remember it, and that only made her shiver harder.

She decided she had to get her mind off of it.

She stood up from her spot at the furnace, blanket ends hovering at her ankles like a great, multi-layered shawl. Parenti immediately reacted, made a move like to catch her, though she hadn't stumbled.

"I'm fine," she said, shooing him away. Her legs weren't asleep anymore. The pins and needles she was feeling was proof enough of that. She thought it was probably good that she was feeling them, and so she embraced it, leaned into them as she hobbled across the furnace bay, to where Felix stood.

His eyes were on the strange-looking density gun in his hands—a flamethrower, they'd told her—but they looked up as she approached, then widened.

"Oh—" he said.

Margo had hugged him. "Thank you," she said, squeezing him tight before letting go. "I couldn't have lasted in there much longer."

"Me neither," said Lumen, still wrapped in her own blanket by the heater.

"Nor could I," said Parenti with a nod.

Uncomfortable as always amidst the attention, Felix dipped his head down, let his hair hang over his eyes as he scratched at the back of his neck.

"Don't mention it." He shrugged.

Margo found herself smirking. He was a strange kid, Felix, but he'd saved them. He'd saved them all.

Her smile fell. Almost all.

She turned to Parenti, to where he sat at the nearest corner computer, eyes fixed on the screen.

"Anything?" she asked, careful not to let anything tinge her voice, hope or fear.

"Yeah," Parenti said, looking up slowly. "I found him."

The look on his face was enough to break her heart, to make the cold that gripped her turn suddenly eternal. She forced herself to ask anyway, voice cracking as she did. "And?"

Parenti's face was like stone. "He—Casper...he didn't make it."

Margo's breath caught in her throat. She felt her knees go weak as the weight of his words fell upon her, and as the tears began to well up.

Don't cry, she told herself. *Not yet*. But the tears weren't listening, were already clouding her vision, streaming down her cheeks. She wiped them away with cold fingers, felt a sob choking its way up her throat.

A loud bang made her forget it, sent Felix jumping on her left. It was followed in the next second by another, and then three more in quick succession.

"What the—?" Lumen said, jumping to her feet, head darting around for the source.

Margo had already found it.

"The space hatch," she said, motioning ahead.

The furnace bay space hatch was one of three exits on the Phenomena 7. It was operated by an old-school wheel in its center and led directly to the outside.

To the space beyond.

"Someone's out there?" Lumen said incredulously, pulling something out of her own blanket shawl. It looked like some kind of metal pipe.

"Some*thing*," Margo said. Something that wanted in. She'd already pulled out her density gun, had trained it on the door. Beside her, Felix had done the same with his flamethrower.

"Parenti, can you get a visual on the feeds?"

She saw him shake his head in the peripheral. "No," he said, frantically tapping keys. "The outer cameras are still offline. I can't tell what—"

A hard click cut off his words. The wheel on the exit's front had rotated. The hatch had been unlocked.

"Oh *hell* no," Lumen said, readying her pipe to swing.

Beside her, Margo heard Felix swallow hard.

They all watched as slowly, the door lurched open.

What fell through was a humanoid thing, with blue skin and a large, abnormally shaped head.

Lumen immediately let out a war cry, raising her pipe to beat the thing to a pulp. At the same time, Margo heard the unmistakable hiss of flame as Felix prepared to scorch the intruder with a blast of fire. Had she reacted a second sooner, Margo might have fired too, though something made her wait, and at the last second, she saw it.

"*Wait!*" she screamed, and she dove forward, putting herself in the way of both pipe and flame.

"Margo, move!" Lumen said. "It's another one! Another Amygdalom!"

"No!" Margo said, waving her arms frantically. The motion caused her blanket shawl to fall off her shoulders, and the cold which swept in threatened to take her voice away. "No it's—"

But the intruder was dusting off its shoulders now, and its face too. Wiping off white frost and ice crystals to reveal a blue skin underneath. A blue uniform. It hit a button on its belt, pulled back the nanonylon helmet that had encased its abnormally shaped head. Or rather, the head that had only looked abnormal because it had a coffee mug birthday hat on top of it.

It was Casper.

He took a step forward, looked like he was about to say something, but stumbled before he could.

Margo caught him before he hit the ground.

They all did.

"Casper!" she cried, holding him with the entire crew. "Oh, Casper, are you all right?" New tears were falling down her face now. Good tears.

Casper didn't respond for a moment, looked even colder than Margo felt, though he was slowly coming to. His eyes met hers. "Margo? I—"

Margo kissed him before he could finish. She couldn't help herself.

He looked surprised at first, but he soon smiled. "Margo, I did it," he said.

"Did what?" she said, smiling despite herself, tears running hot down her cool face.

He raised a finger, pointed to the coffee mug still upside down on his head. "I kept it on," he said. "I kept my birthday hat on all day."

Margo laughed, a gross, snotty laugh that was probably halfway to a sob and pulled him tight to her. And though she was still freezing, though the touch of Casper's space-chilled skin didn't help, at that moment, Margo felt warmer than she ever had.

ACKNOWLEDGMENTS

Thank you to those awesome folk I have the privilege of calling my friends and family. It is their continued love and support of me that make all the special parts of life sweeter, and all the scary ones less so.

ALSO BY KIERAN WIESENBERG

The Arcane Amnesiac

ABOUT THE AUTHOR

Kieran Wiesenberg is an indie author from western New York. Find out more at kieranwiesenberg.com

www.ingramcontent.com/pod-product-compliance
Lightning Source LLC
Chambersburg PA
CBHW072034170626
46811CB00008B/3078